VAMPIRIC
VACATION

ALSO IN THE SINISTER SUMMER SERIES

Wretched Waterpark

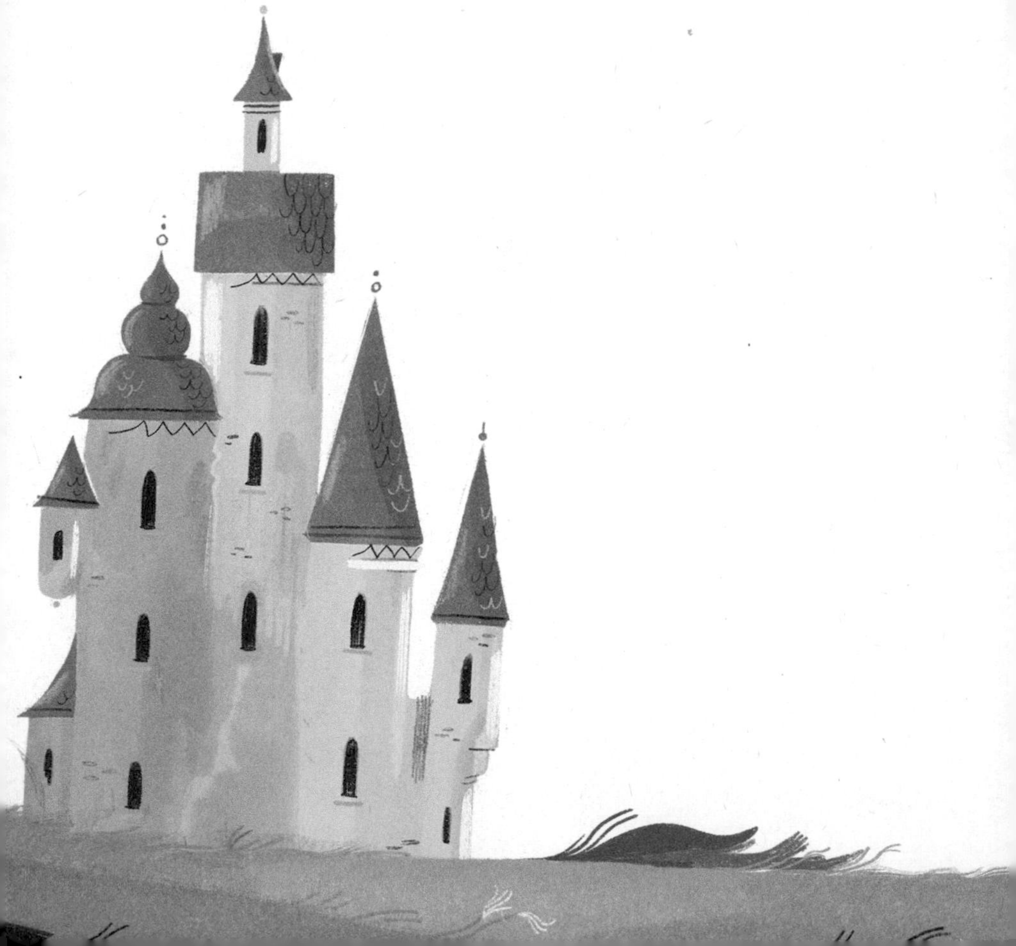

VAMPIRIC VACATION

The Sinister Summer Series

KIERSTEN WHITE

DELACORTE PRESS

Text copyright © 2022 by Kiersten Brazier
Jacket art copyright © 2022 by Hannah Peck

rhcbooks.com

Educators and librarians, for a variety of teaching tools, visit us at RHTeachersLibrarians.com

Library of Congress Cataloging-in-Publication Data is available upon request.
ISBN 978-0-593-37908-0 (hardcover) — ISBN 978-0-593-37909-7 (lib. bdg.) — ISBN 978-0-593-37910-3 (ebook) — ISBN 978-0-593-64490-4 (int'l. ed.)

The text of this book is set in 12.75-point Adobe Jenson Pro.
Interior design by Jen Valero

Printed in the United States of America
10 9 8 7 6 5 4 3 2 1
First Edition

For all the kids who can't stop fidgeting:
Same. Come sit by me.

lexander unlocked Wil's door, and they crept inside. The drapes were pulled tightly, the entire space as dim as a haunted graveyard at twilight. Wil was cocooned in her blankets, not even her face visible.

"You do the drapes; I'll garlic her," Theo whispered.

"Are we sure about this?" Alexander had never considered what it might take to save a teenage sister from undead existence. Were they making the right choice?

"It has to be done," Theo said, her voice solemn but determined. No evil vampires were taking her sister away. "We do it on the count of three."

Alexander nodded. He took the drapes firmly in hand, watching over his shoulder. "One . . ." Theo unscrewed the lid to the garlic salt.

"Two . . . ," Alexander whispered, bracing himself as though he were at the start of a race and didn't know what the finish line would bring.

"Three!"

Alexander flung open the drapes. Wil sat up, the blankets falling away from her face as she blinked bleary red eyes at them.

"Yaaaargh!" Theo shouted, and threw the whole bottle of garlic salt.

Wil screamed, clawing at her face.

Had they just saved their sister . . . or destroyed her?

CHAPTER
ONE

The day was decidedly sinister.

But not in a charming Sinister-Winterbottom way. If it was a Sinister-Winterbottom way, it might be a day that puttered around the yard building battle robots with built-in cookie ovens, like Mr. Sinister-Winterbottom.

Or it might be a day that painted wild murals of storm-tossed seas populated with tentacled friends while its cookies baked in the battle-robot oven, like Ms. Sinister-Winterbottom.

Or it might be a day with its nose against a phone screen while a frown creased its impressively expressive black eyebrows, like Wilhelmina Sinister-Winterbottom.

Or it might be a day that ran at full speed, the wind whipping its hair, grass lashing its bare shins, screaming joy and delight and something close to anger, like Theodora Sinister-Winterbottom.

Or it might be a day that gazed pensively out the car window at the blurring landscape, wondering what it was heading toward and what might possibly go wrong there because it couldn't imagine that everything would just be fun and pleasant and *nothing* would go wrong, like Alexander Sinister-Winterbottom.

Well . . . on second thought, this day *was* rather like Alexander Sinister-Winterbottom.

Heavy clouds pressed down on the atmosphere, looming closer than clouds ought to loom, as though they were worried about the day, too, and couldn't keep it to themselves. They scooted closer and closer to the earth, peering down at the massive aqua car drifting at alarming speed down a lonely road.

"Pretty dark for noon," Alexander said, unable to swallow the tight lump of worry stuck in his throat. He loved storms—from his own house, curled up on the window seat, with a mug of hot cocoa and a good book, and his mother humming somewhere deep under the house

4

while his father scrambled to get all the battle robots into the garage. But he didn't have his window seat, or hot cocoa, or a good book, or his parents. And he still didn't know why he and his siblings had been banished to spend the summer with their mysterious aunt Saffronia.

Theo repeatedly bonked her head against the cold glass of the car window, like the world's worst drum. She hated long car rides. She couldn't read without getting sick, so she usually listened to an audiobook, but there was no stereo, just a weird old radio you had to adjust by twisting knobs. Aunt Saffronia seemed happy to keep the knobs between stations. The maddening white noise of static filled the car. Every once in a while, Theo could *swear* she heard voices whispering in the static, just barely too quiet to understand.

Which made her mad, because there was already so much she didn't understand right now. Why had their parents woken them in the middle of the night and dumped them on Aunt Saffronia a week ago? Why hadn't their parents at least called since then? Why did she feel both angry and sad at the same time, when she didn't want to feel either, and why did these big feelings make her buzz like she was filled with a hive of angry bees?

Holding her head against the window made her skull vibrate and her teeth chatter. It was as close as she could get to moving while stuck in a car, so she pressed her forehead harder against the glass. This drive seemed like it had lasted forever.

Had they even gone back to Aunt Saffronia's house after leaving Fathoms of Fun Waterpark? Theo glanced at Alexander. He wasn't in his swimsuit, and they were both totally dry. They must have gone back to their aunt's house, showered, and changed. But . . . Theo couldn't remember doing any of that. They had been in the car at Fathoms of Fun, and now they were in the car going somewhere else, and her brain couldn't connect the dots about what had happened between.

"Weird," she muttered, bonking her head once more against the window.

Alexander didn't need to know what Theo thought was weird. Everything was weird, and he didn't like it, and his stomach hurt with all the not-liking he was doing regarding all the weird they were experiencing.

In the passenger seat, Wil, age sixteen and therefore four years older than twins Alexander and Theo, and therefore permanently claiming shotgun in the unfair way older siblings always do—as though a few extra years on earth put them first in line for everything, forever— paused her frantic typing on her phone when a message popped up.

"Edgar," she said, a dreamy smile breaking the intensely focused expression on her face.

"Edgar?" Alexander and Theo said at the same time, perking up. Edgar was a lifeguard at the water park they had just left after a week of fun.

Well . . . after two days of fun. Before the two days of fun were several days of wily Widows, menacing mustaches, terrifying tunnels, and lingering in libraries. Most of their time at Fathoms of Fun had been rather stressful and occasionally scary, thanks to an evil fraternal twin and her henchman. But it ended on a rush of reuniting the real Widows and restoring the park to its Gothic glory. And since it all ended happily, the three Sinister-Winterbottoms only felt happy when they thought of it.

Of course, Wil felt a *little* more than happy when Edgar texted her.

And who could say what Aunt Saffronia felt? Her face was still oddly indistinct, as though seen through several panes of thick glass. Her gaze never seemed to focus on what was around her. Except for right now, as she turned and stared at the antique brass stopwatch Theo still wore around her neck.

"Umm," Alexander said.

"Aunt Saffronia?" Theo added.

"You should be watching the road!" Wil said, which was sharp criticism coming from a girl who never looked up from her phone.

"I should?" Aunt Saffronia tilted her head, her long black hair moving in slow motion, as though she were trapped underwater.

Theo had a strange moment of wondering if Aunt Saffronia really did need to watch the road, though. The car was still going perfectly straight, as though it was steering itself. But that was impossible. A car so old that it didn't even have a good stereo certainly couldn't have a self-driving option . . . could it?

"Please keep your eyes on the road!" Alexander squeaked, a hundred different ways the car could crash all crashing through his head.

Aunt Saffronia laughed, a sound like wind chimes. Not tinkling, bright metal wind chimes, but old chimes, made of wood, so they just sort of brushed and clacked against each other. "Silly boy," she said. "If my eyes were on the road, that would really scare you. I'll keep them in my head." Then she paused, turning ever so slowly to look straight out the windshield. "Unless children like that sort of thing?"

Alexander and Theo exchanged a baffled look. Though they were twins, they were hardly mirror images. Theo had brown hair, cut short so she wouldn't have to worry about brushing it. It was pushed back from her forehead by a headband that made it stick up wildly, rather hedgehog-like in appearance.

Alexander's hair was also cut very short, but not so short that he didn't have to comb it. He still combed it, very carefully, every morning, and often several times during the day. Like Theo, he had brown eyes, and freckles across his nose. Unlike Theo's, his knees were not covered in bruises and scars, and also unlike Theo, he had managed to spend an entire week at a water park and not get sunburned at all. His white skin was still very white.

Theo, meanwhile, scratched her shoulders, where a sunburn nagged at her.

Wil was also not sunburned, her brown skin perfectly protected since she spent most of the time at the water park doing the same thing she did with most of her time everywhere else: gazing at Rodrigo, her beloved phone.

Though, increasingly, it looked like what Rodrigo's small screen showed her didn't make her happy. Already the smile at a text from Edgar was gone, replaced with a frustrated frown as she idly tugged on one of her many long braids. If their father were here, he would gently remind Wil not to pull her hair.

But their father wasn't here, so Wil's hair had no one to look out for it.

"Where are we going?" Theo asked. "And when will we get there? And when are our parents coming to get us?"

"And aren't we going to stop at the house to pick up our things? Or is this just a day trip? Or are we going to meet our parents?" Alexander couldn't help but sound hopeful at that last question.

Unfortunately, Aunt Saffronia was very good at only hearing the questions she wanted to hear. "We aren't finished yet."

"With the drive? Or the vacation?" Alexander asked, desperate for some sort of clarity. All he remembered about being dropped off with Aunt Saffronia was that it had been in the middle of the night. His mom was trying hard to sound cheery, but her eyes were worried, and his father had been hastily packing several of his most impressive robots. They had also, for some reason, lit a lot of candles in a circle. And that was it.

Since then, the only contact they'd had with their parents was a letter left in Alexander's luggage. His mom had a way of packing that was like magic—every time Alexander opened the suitcase, he found exactly what he needed, whether it was an extra pair of board shorts, or his softest sleep shirt, or extra floss, because cavities never take a summer vacation. So when Alexander had found the letter from his mom, he'd thought it was what he needed: Answers. Explanations. A scavenger hunt that would end with his being reunited with his parents.

Instead, he had found a letter telling him to be cautious, Theo to be brave, and Wil to use her phone. All it had said about Aunt Saffronia was that they should listen to her, except when they shouldn't. And something about gathering tools. Which seemed weird, since they weren't at home with their dad, who was forever losing his robot-building materials.

Alexander sighed, feeling squeezed by impending stormy doom. Aunt Saffronia wasn't going to tell him anything. She was just like most adults, barreling through the world, never explaining the baffling things going on around them.

Theo didn't give up on answers so easily. Maybe if she broke the sentences down, one question at a time, it would help Aunt Saffronia. Sometimes if a teacher gave Theo too many instructions at once, she couldn't figure out which task to do first, so she ended up doing none of them and instead building an elaborate tower out of pencils, glue sticks, and erasers. Her mom was really good at helping Theo organize her brain, which only had one speed: *fast*.

But she would slow it down to try to get answers from Aunt Saffronia.

"Where are we?" Theo asked.

"In the car." Aunt Saffronia sighed worriedly. "They told me you children were bright, that you could do this, but sometimes I wonder. It's a lot to ask of any child, much less one who can't understand when she's inside a car."

Theo resisted the urge to tug on her own hair. "Where are we going?"

"Nowhere," Aunt Saffronia said. "We're already here." The car stopped abruptly. It had been moving so fast that the landscape was a blur, and now it was stopped, and none of the three children could remember the jolt, or even the gradual slowing. But that was quickly forgotten by the alarm they felt at what they were reading. Usually reading was a pleasant task for Alexander and Theo, but it didn't feel pleasant as they looked at the sign in front of them:

WELCOME TO THE LITTLE TRANSYLVANIAN MOUNTAINS
WE ARE DYING TO MEET YOU

CHAPTER
TWO

"Is it just me," Alexander said, "or does that sign seem—"

"Ominous?" Theo suggested.

"Vaguely threatening?" Alexander added.

"Unaware that 'welcome' and 'dying' don't belong together?"

"Just what we're looking for," Aunt Saffronia said. She pointed. Beyond the welcome sign was another sign.

"'The Sanguine Spa,'" Wil read, flicking her big brown eyes up just long enough to see the words.

"'An all-inclusive family destination,'" Alexander read. That line made him sad, because how could it be all-inclusive for families if their whole family wasn't included?

"If I see so much as a single raisin, I'm revolting,"

Theo grumbled. She had been denied churros at the water park, and threatened with raisin-meat pies. This trip should be full of good food to make up for last week, but she couldn't imagine a spa having churros. Spas were for relaxing, and *relaxing* was grown-up speak for doing things that were healthy and boring. Theo didn't want to eat nutritious food, or talk about her feelings, or sit quietly with her thoughts. That sounded *awful*.

"Go on," Aunt Saffronia said. "You'll be staying here for the week. That should be enough time. And remember: look closer. We need you to look closer."

"But we don't have our stuff," Alexander said. He definitely would have remembered stopping at Aunt Saffronia's house and repacking for another trip.

"Yes, you do."

"Oh," Theo said, staring down at her feet. Next to them, somehow unnoticed before now, were their suitcases. Wil hefted her bag without question, climbing out of the car.

Aunt Saffronia, however, didn't move.

"Wait, aren't you coming?" Alexander found their aunt confusing and a little unnerving, but if he didn't have his parents, he'd at least like adult supervision. Alexander loved adult supervision. It made the world make sense, made everything feel safer, made him certain all the necessary paperwork was going to be filled out correctly.

The back car doors opened. "How does a car without a working radio have a self-driving option and automatic doors?" Theo mused aloud as she tumbled out onto the gravel road, glad to be free.

Alexander stayed in his seat. "You're really not coming?"

Aunt Saffronia shook her head. "It's not my realm. I cannot do this task. Only you can."

Alexander slowly climbed out. He stood next to Theo, who was bouncing up and down with impatience, and Wil, who was staring at Rodrigo.

Aunt Saffronia leaned out her window. They couldn't remember her rolling it down. She stared past them, to a narrow trail winding through the woods. It didn't look like an entrance to a spa, but then again, the Sinister-Winterbottom children had never been to a spa before. "Remember," Aunt Saffronia said. "You need to look closer. And watch each other's necks."

"Don't you mean each other's backs?" Wil muttered, annoyed.

But Aunt Saffronia was already driving away. A bend in the road swallowed her car, and the Sinister-

Winterbottom children were once again left alone, watched only by the looming trees.

And the creatures in those trees, of course. Of which there were many, but none visible to the children.

"Wait," Alexander said. "This is . . . Transylvania?"

Here is a brief Transylvanian history, all of which Theo knew because of a brief obsession with Vlad Dracul, the historic real Romanian prince who inspired the non-historic fictional vampire, Dracula:

Transylvania is in Europe. This fact does not change—like most geographical locations, Transylvania does not periodically pick itself up and settle down for a break on the beach, or for a ski trip, or to visit a baffling and previously unknown aunt. However, *where* Transylvania is in Europe does change because people make borders. A border is an imaginary line, like the one you sometimes draw across the middle of your room to designate which side is yours and which side is your sibling's so that you can get as close as possible to the line and fight about it.

Borders are literally, exactly, that same thing, only for countries instead of siblings.

Transylvania has been Transylvania. It's been Hungary. It's been Wallachia. It's been Romania. It's been Dacia. It's been ruled by Bulgaria, the Ottomans, part of the Habsburg kingdom, part of the Austro-Hungarian empire, and back to Romania. Transylvania's history is like capture the flag and keep-away, with Transylvania being both the flag and the kept-away item.

But through it all, the thing that never changes is that Transylvania is one of the most beautiful places in the world. Deepest green trees; darkest gray rock; soaring mountains cut through with turbulent, winding rivers; fields of green and riots of flowers and medieval stone cities built on hills.

Another thing that never changes is that whoever ruled it, whatever imaginary lines were drawn and erased and drawn again as countries threw tantrums and picked fights and argued over whose turn it was to clean out the closet and whether the tipped-over garbage can was on their side of the room or not, Transylvania remains in exactly the same spot it always has been. Which is in Europe.

Alexander and Theo were 93 percent certain they hadn't somehow traveled to Europe.

"You can't drive to Europe from America, can you?" Alexander asked. He liked to read mythology and mysteries more than nonfiction, and though he had done his homework and memorized all the countries and their capitals in fifth grade, he had since forgotten.

He broke out in a cold sweat. What if this was a quiz, and he really *did* need to know every capital of every country in the world, and now he was going to be in trouble, or take a wrong turn and accidentally end up in Europe? He was sure his parents, who didn't like them going to play at neighbors' houses without permission, would definitely not like them going to play on another *continent* without permission.

Theo preferred nonfiction. A few years ago, before her Vlad Dracul phase, she had gone through a bridges-and-underwater-tunnels phase, much as other children go through cowboy phases, or anime phases, or learning-to-hack-into-top-secret-databases-using-only-their-cell-phone phases.

"No," Theo said, quite confident that there was no way to drive from America to Europe. "We are definitely not in the real Transylvania. But sometimes when people move into new areas that remind them of old areas, they rename the areas after where they came from."

"Like taking home with you wherever you go," Alexander said, wishing he could literally do that.

Though the Sinister-Winterbottoms had never traveled to Transylvania, they could still appreciate the towering green trees. Beneath their branches, ferns fidgeted in the breeze. A slug the size of Theo's thumb slimed sluggishly along the path in front of them, yellow racing stripes going down its black body like a false promise of speed.

"Why doesn't Aunt Saffronia ever walk us in?" Wil grumbled. "The least she could do is handle check-in. I'm busy."

"Busy with what?" Theo demanded, since Wil was as busy as she ever was, which is to say, not busy at all but just glued to her phone.

"Actually," Alexander said, "the least Aunt Saffronia could do is watch us, since our parents asked her to, you know, *watch* us." He tugged the collar of his shirt, adjusting his grip on his suitcase. Though it was shady beneath all the big trees, the day was still muggy. He almost longed for the unearthly chill of the cave at the Cold, Unknowable Sea wave pool back at Fathoms of Fun. Almost, but not quite.

But now that Alexander had started worrying, he couldn't stop. It happened that way a lot. A single prickling spike of worry turned into a whole cactus of them.

"It's a family spa," he said. "What if they don't let us in without an adult because we aren't a complete family? We could be stranded here." Alexander gazed into the trees, picking out which one he would sleep under. But then he started imagining the slugs sliming over him in his sleep, and then he started wondering what else was creeping out there. Just because all he had seen were slugs didn't mean there weren't other animals.

And Alexander was very right. There were, in fact, other animals he couldn't see, and wouldn't see until nightfall. And even then, it would be awfully difficult for him to see them, though *they* would see *him*. . . .

"Come on." Theo would actually have liked the idea of sleeping outside in the woods, had such a thing occurred to her. But she was focused on checking in, which sounded long and boring, so they could get to whatever activities there were at a spa, which also sounded boring. But unlike Alexander, she held out hope that *something* would be fun.

Wil, eyes glued to Rodrigo, began walking straight into the woods. Theo took her arm and steered her toward the pathway. "What are you even doing on that stupid thing?" Theo asked. Sometimes she got jealous of Rodrigo like it was a person, not a lifeless phone. Even though Theo knew she was Wil's favorite sister—only sister, which also made her Wil's least favorite sister, but Theo ignored that fact—it bugged her that Wil gave all her attention to Rodrigo.

"Looking," Wil said.

"Like Aunt Saffronia told us to?" Alexander asked, still unable to shake that oh-no-I-missed-a-school-assignment feeling. "She told us to look closer. What did she mean by that?"

At Fathoms of Fun, she had told them to find what was lost and that they needed time. It turned out she didn't care at all about the missing park owner. She just wanted them to find the stopwatch Theo now wore. Alexander had hoped it was part of their annual family scavenger hunt, but without their parents here, they could hardly have a family scavenger hunt. Still, he wondered why Aunt Saffronia had been so happy to see the timer.

Theo's mind was on the same track. While very different children, Theo and Alexander often had similar thoughts as a result of being together from birth. Theo sighed wistfully. When someone is full of wist, they want something they don't have. In this case, it was the same thing Alexander wanted: their whole family, together, on a scavenger hunt. She rubbed the stopwatch thoughtfully. "Remember the year we had to add all the birth and death dates on the Sinister gravestones in the cemetery to get to a number that turned out to be the GPS coordinates where Mom and Dad buried treasure?"

"I liked that one," Wil said, shocking them because she was actually listening. That hunt, Wil had done all the math in her head, no calculator app needed. Theo had plotted out the coordinates on the map. And Alexander had created elaborate backstories—and occasionally funny poems—based on the names of the graves they had to visit.

"Me too," Alexander and Theo said.

"Well, come on." Wil hiked her backpack up higher on her back. Alexander dragged his suitcase. And Theo kept her eyes out for the best climbing trees, even though no one asked her to.

"I wonder who made this trail?" Alexander asked. It wasn't paved, but it looked well used. He had a nagging worry that this was all a big joke and they were on a long hiking trail to nowhere. But Aunt Saffronia didn't seem like a practical joker.

Still, spas were supposed to be fancy, right? This trail

wasn't fancy. It was hugged by trees and ferns, each creeping in closer, as if to convince the trail it didn't really want to lead children to their destination, but rather deeper and deeper into the woods, never to return. It made no sense that it would lead to a spa. What if Aunt Saffronia had left them at the wrong place?

"Is that it?" Theo asked, pointing. She wasn't particularly anxious to get to the spa, but she could tell Alexander was and she wanted to be helpful. They had only been walking for eight minutes and twenty-seven seconds—she was timing it—but when you didn't know where you were going, paths felt a lot longer than they actually were. Time was funny that way. Always warping to move either faster or slower, usually the opposite of whichever way you wanted it to move. That was one of the reasons Theo loved her timer so much. She could capture time, keep it ticking along precisely how it should.

"What?" Alexander asked, trying to figure out what Theo was seeing. There were no buildings, nothing that said *spa*. There were only infinite trees making it impossible to see more than a few feet ahead of them, and a jumble of large boulders to the right of the path, hugging the edge of a drop-off.

Alexander narrowed his eyes, confused by what he

was seeing. A jumble of large boulders . . . with a small metal door set into one of the boulders, complete with a keypad for entering a code.

It couldn't possibly be the spa. There were no signs around it, no welcome mat. And no one would ever even notice it unless they were keeping a sharp eye out for climbing opportunities. Most people didn't walk down random paths in the Little Transylvania woods looking for things to climb. (Unless they were hoping that climbing would somehow keep them safe. But of course it wouldn't. So many things that would chase you in the woods could also climb or never needed to climb at all to reach high places.)

"I wonder—" Alexander started, but then he shouted in dismay. Because Wil wasn't wondering. She was wandering, nose to her phone, right toward the cliff edge.

CHAPTER
THREE

Alexander and Theo dropped their suitcases, grabbed Wil's backpack, and yanked her so she fell hard onto her behind. "Hey!" she shouted, outraged. "You almost made me drop Rodrigo!"

"And Rodrigo almost made you drop off a cliff!" Alexander couldn't stop himself from imagining Wil falling. He put a hand over his chest, trying to stop his heart from racing. But he couldn't find the finish line for his fear. The fear just kept running and running through him, filling his mind with terrible images.

He closed his eyes and, remembering a trick his mom taught him for when his brain was racing out of control, said, "Stop," out loud to himself.

Theo, who wasn't struggling with her thoughts and quite liked the thrill of heights, walked to the edge and peered down. "Lots of nice rocks to break your fall down there, Wil." From this angle, the cliff face looked downright climbable, and Theo couldn't help but feel a surge of excitement. Maybe that's why there was a path here! It led to the cliff because one of the spa activities was climbing! Or the *opposite* of climbing, which in this case was not falling, but controlled-falling-on-purpose-with-ropes. Theo had always wanted to go rappelling. "Come on! Let's check in!" She grabbed Alexander's hand to hurry him along.

He appreciated it because Theo tugging him helped tug his brain away from its catastrophic thoughts of cliffs and disasters and slugs and sleeping outside and rolling off a cliff in his sleep into a nest of slugs. Did slugs make nests? What would they do if someone disturbed their nest?

"Is it just me," Theo said, "or is Wil even more intense about her phone than usual?"

"We'll have to keep a better eye on her," Alexander said. He felt responsible, even though he was the youngest by a few seconds—he and Theo were born hand in hand, but as usual, she went first.

Theo and Alexander went around an old dead tree that had fallen across the path. "Wil," Theo called, waiting for Wil to stumble up to them. Wil neither went around nor leaped over the tree, instead bumping into it and then awkwardly scrambling over. "Why don't you look up the spa? See how close we are?"

"Busy," Wil said. But at least she followed them, managing to avoid any further close calls with cliffs.

Theo forged ahead, with Alexander keeping a nervous hand on Wil's elbow. But the trail soon came to an abrupt stop that puzzled them all.

Instead of delivering them to a hotel or spa, the small dirt path led them to a narrow gap between two towering hedges. The hedges were so high they blocked the view of anything other than the sky. The branches were densely packed, with leaves a dark, waxy green, each point delicate and sharp, as though just waiting for someone to touch them and learn their lesson. It was impossible to push through or climb.

Alexander looked up and down, but the woods were thick and the hedge was right up against them. There were no other trails besides the one they came in on. He didn't see any way around it.

"This must be the way in?" Theo said, puzzled. She stepped inside and looked one direction, then the other. The ground here was covered with gravel, like a reflection of the gray of the clouds above them. This was a carefully tended path, which was confusing since it didn't seem to lead anywhere. And if Theo took a few steps, she wouldn't even be able to see the narrow gap where she had entered. She'd be lost.

She looked back at her siblings. "I think this is a maze." Her heart started beating faster. But not because she was worried or scared or wondering when they would find food and indoor toilets, like Alexander was. No, her heart was beating faster because she was excited. She loved mazes. And, unlike the tunnels beneath Fathoms of Fun, which were merely maze*like*, this was a proper, honest-to-goodness, who-took-the-time-to-make-this? maze!

"Turn right!" she commanded, marching confidently forward.

Alexander complied, continuing to lead Wil by her elbow. Theo made two more right turns before they hit a dead end. She marched back and made a left turn instead of the last right. When she hit a dead end, she backtracked. And when she hit another dead end, she backtracked again, slowly building a map in her head of where they had been in hopes of finding where they were supposed to go.

She could do this all day.

Alexander didn't feel the same way. So it was with no small amount of relief that he noticed something. "Look!" he said. "The gravel is sort of disturbed here." It looked like tiny feet had walked on the current path they were taking.

Theo frowned, dubious. "Looks like footprints from a little kid. Who's to say they know the way through any better than I do?"

"Let's at least try, okay?" Alexander was anxious to get out. What if they missed the check-in and were denied rooms? What if they missed the check-in and were denied *bathrooms?* Unfortunately, Alexander had fallen into the cruelest trap nature ever designed: worrying about whether or not you needed to go to the bathroom when there were no bathrooms available was an absolute guaranteed way to make yourself need to go to the bathroom.

Annoyed, Theo stomped along the footsteps' trail. A few times she thought she lost it—and didn't mind because she really did want to solve this on her own—but inevitably Alexander would find a hint of it. He was good at finding things, and also very, very motivated.

In the center of the maze, they came to a small, circular clearing. There was a fountain there, the stone dry, whatever water might have burbled to make the scene pleasant long since turned off. The fountain statue at first glance looked like a person draped in cloth and wearing a hat with two big points. Until they looked closer and realized it was, in fact, a giant bat wrapped in its own wings, towering over them, looking down with fangs bared.

"I . . . don't like that," Alexander said.

"Look! The footprints!" Theo barely noticed the statue since it didn't really change the maze one way or another. She would definitely come back and do it all again on her own, but for Alexander's sake, she was treating the footprints like the lines on a treasure map. They followed the prints for a few more twists and turns and corners, and then, as quickly as they were swallowed by the maze, they went through an arched opening and were dumped out onto an unexpectedly manicured lawn.

There were nets for badminton games, a volleyball court, a ropes course, even a pool. Though Alexander had had enough of pools and water for a while. "No waves!"

Theo and Alexander said at the same time, one of them disappointed, one of them relieved, not a mystery at all which emotion belonged to which twin. There was, however, a waterslide with an eerily familiar gargoyle face at the top.

"Same designer?" Alexander mused, trying not to be nervous. Fathoms of Fun had ended up being fun after all, even if it had a lot of *scary* before it was fun.

Theo was too excited to notice the gargoyle. Wild woods, big cliffs, a maze, plus a ropes course and games and a pool! The spa was looking better and better. At least, what they could see of it, which was only a lawn so far. The hedge maze lurked behind them, separating the spa grounds from the woods. Alexander gently redirected Wil away from where she was about to walk straight back into the greenery.

"I wonder how long it would take her to find her way out if we let her go in alone?" Theo asked.

"I wonder how long it would take her to even notice she was in a maze," Alexander added.

"Yeah, amazing," Wil mumbled in a distracted attempt to show she was paying attention. The twins each took one of Wil's elbows and turned her, but they were so shocked at what they saw that they accidentally yanked her arms.

"Hey!" Wil shouted, Rodrigo dropping to the ground. "Watch it, twerps!"

But they were too busy looking to watch, or to look down and see what, exactly, Wil was doing on her phone. If they had, they would have had a lot more questions than answers, the first question being: Why was Wil looking up ancient obituaries, notes newspapers printed about people who died?

Theo and Alexander only had eyes for the spa that loomed in front of them, though *spa* felt like the wrong name. If anything, it looked like a castle. It was made of the same dark gray rocks that dominated the spaces between the trees, and it dominated this space in much the same way. The center had a tower with a spire that seemed likely to puncture the clouds and dump rain on all of them. The walls of the spa went up and up, with spikes and turrets trying to take a bite out of the sky. Narrow windows looked out, suspicious of these newcomers traipsing across their lawn.

Alexander noted with relief that there did not appear to be anyone behind the glass in the tower window, or any of the other windows, for that matter.

"No Widows in sight," Theo said, nudging him.

Alexander nodded. "This place looks—"

"Cool?" Theo suggested.

"It looks—"

"Promising?"

"It looks . . . unsettling," Alexander settled on. Because even though there was no one behind the glass, he couldn't get over the feeling that the windows were watching him.

CHAPTER
FOUR

"Edgar says the spa is fun," Wil said, nearly walking right into the pool but adjusting her course at the last possible moment. Alexander and Theo scurried to catch up.

"He's been here?" That made Alexander feel better. Edgar liked it, and Alexander liked Edgar, so it stood to reason Alexander might like it here.

"Is he coming?" Theo asked. She liked Edgar, too. Though neither of them *like* liked Edgar, like Wil did.

"No." Wil didn't sound happy about it. "Too much work at Fathoms of Fun now that there are customers again."

They walked around the spa, looking for an entrance.

It was a very large building, all by itself, in the middle of a cliff-filled forest. Like someone had been playing a video game, cleared one square of trees to create the most epic and creepily huge building possible, and then walked away.

At last, they reached the front. They had gotten so used to the quiet solitude of the forest that it was a shock to find themselves staring at a line of cars and a line of people, one spewing impatient exhaust and the other spewing impatient exhaustion.

"Hurry up!" one man snapped at his son, who was dragging three large suitcases out of the trunk of their car. "We're behind schedule already! I had planned on having a full hour of relaxation by now!"

His son, a boy around the twins' age, heaved the last suitcase free. "We'll have to relax twice as hard to make up for it." He frowned. "But if we relax hard, does that make it not relaxing?"

"Stop being silly and come on!" The man pushed inside past a mother doing a head count of her four children.

"One, two, three, four. Did we always have four kids?" she asked, eyes wide with surprise. "That seems like such a lot of children! What were we thinking?"

Her four kids shrugged. They went down in a line, decreasing in size like the bars on Wil's cell phone coverage.

"Russian nesting dolls," Alexander whispered to Theo. She giggled, trying to hide her laugh behind her hand because she wasn't sure if it was rude. But Alexander had a point. If you could have opened up the oldest child—which you should never do because children should remain firmly closed—you could have slipped the second oldest inside, on and on down to the smallest one, who would have nestled in the center.

Behind the nesting-doll family were a tall mom and a short dad unbuckling two very small children from car seats so elaborate it would take even a professional escape artist ages to undo everything. The dad was sweating, and the mom was muttering words under her breath that Alexander was quite certain he wasn't allowed to say. "How is everything sticky?" the dad asked.

His wide-eyed toddler lifted her sippy cup and held it upside down, watching it slowly, slowly drip on her father's desperate hands as he tried to find the last strap to unbuckle. Her brother, a slightly larger toddler, pulled a sucker out of his mouth and gently placed it in their mother's hair.

"Where did he even get a sucker?" their mom cried,

throwing her hands up in surrender. "I can't undo all these straps!"

The toddler went limp like a jellyfish and somehow wriggled free all on his own. Even professional escape artists cannot beat toddlers wriggling free of things meant to contain them, which is why escape artists are some of the strongest advocates for making child labor illegal. They just can't handle the competition.

"They're not doing a very good job of wrangling," someone said. Theo turned to see a girl around their own age. Her hair was long and black, much like her eyes, which were black but not long, as eyes rarely are. Also unlike her eyes, her hair was done in two tight braids trailing down from her rather large cowboy hat. She had a length of rope in her hands, which she twisted and knotted without looking at what she was doing. "Do you think they need help?" She hurried away to where the larger toddler was taking advantage of his parents' distraction to wander away into the woods.

"This is . . . a lot," Alexander said. After a week at Fathoms of Fun with almost no lines at all, having to wait in a chaotic line just to get inside the spa was a bit of a letdown.

Theo could barely stand it. She hated waiting. It was

the most boring thing she could imagine. And they weren't even waiting in line for the ropes course or a churro stand or something worthwhile like that. They were waiting in line to check in to a hotel, which wasn't even fun.

"Too many people," Theo grumbled. She'd probably have to take turns rappelling.

Alexander didn't like having to wait, either, but he *was* comforted by the presence of so many parents. It wasn't going to be a weird vacation like Fathoms of Fun, fending for themselves in a nearly abandoned water park. It was just going to be a normal spa week.

Whatever a normal spa week was. He didn't actually know. His parents had never gone to a spa that he knew of, and they had certainly never taken him.

"It's like they just . . . don't even exist anymore," Wil muttered to herself. "I can't track their phones, their credit cards aren't being used, and they don't respond to anything."

"Who?" Theo went up on her tiptoes to see past the nesting-doll family and figure out how far they were from the check-in desk. The sooner they got checked in, the sooner she could check out—check out the pool, the maze, the rappelling options.

Wil, predictably, didn't acknowledge the question.

Asking Wil direct questions, or telling her something while she was lost in Rodrigo, was like opening up the fridge and shouting your hopes and dreams. Sure, the milk and butter and eggs and leftover pizza were physically there, but they definitely didn't hear you or care about what you said. But at least there was leftover pizza in that scenario.

Alexander was busy looking for a brochure or a map or something he could study. He hadn't noticed the map of Fathoms of Fun and had thus missed out on the library for the first few days. Surely a place like this had a library! And maybe a theater room. He also wanted to tour the kitchens, to make sure their food preparation was safe and their chefs were all certified with local health and safety boards. The food at Fathoms of Fun had been safe but not edible. He was hoping for both safe *and* edible here.

At last, they crossed the threshold of the huge brass doors and entered the lobby. The interior was blessedly cool after the muggy, pre-storm heat outside.

Imagining a spa, Theo had pictured a lot of white furniture, steel, and glass. All modern and sleek and grown-up-ish, just waiting to be smudged.

This was not that.

The floors were dark wood, the walls wood planks, all the furniture made of wood and upholstered with velvet. Normally this much wood would look rustic, but everything was polished, every molding carved, every arm of every chair lovingly shaped with whirls and flourishes and, frequently, a wolf head on a dragon body. It definitely wasn't modern, and wasn't even rustic so much as aggressively impressive. The ceiling soared far overhead, dark beams crisscrossing above an elaborate chandelier, where real candles were burning.

Theo thought the chandelier was cool. Alexander thought it was a fire hazard. Wil never looked up, so she had no opinion on it whatsoever.

"Is the chandelier made of . . . bones?" Alexander asked, craning his neck to stare at it.

"Maybe antlers," Theo said. With the cavernous space so dark and dim, secrets seemed to hide in every corner behind the stir of a velvet curtain or beneath the twist of a wolf's smile. It felt almost like walking onto a movie set. A movie that Alexander would make an excuse to leave the room during instead of watching, and that Theo would happily watch, knowing she wouldn't be able to sleep for a week.

In the center of the lobby, resting on a deep red rug

like an island in a pool of something that was deep red and best not thought about too much, stood an imposing desk, behind which stood a less imposing girl. She looked around Wil's age, with olive-toned skin and dark hair. Her eyes were opened wide, like she was about to scream, but her smile remained firmly in place as she listened to criticisms of the chaos of check-in, took down information, and handed out keys.

The line moved up, and up, and finally the Sinister-Winterbottoms were at the desk.

"Hi," the girl said. Her name tag, old brass like the huge front doors, said *MINA*. She wore a white blouse with a high collar, a black vest with thin purple stripes that buttoned tightly down to a flaring, full black skirt trimmed with purple lace. "Do you have a reservation?"

Wil didn't look up from Rodrigo. "Hmm? I don't know."

"Is that okay?" Alexander felt panic rising. Aunt Saffronia didn't make a reservation! They were going to be turned away! They would have to sleep in the woods! The slugs were probably already circling in anticipation, just waiting for him.

Mina smiled at Alexander, her face finally relaxing into a real smile instead of the I'm-smiling-because-it's-my-job-to-smile-but-really-I-want-to-throw-this-clipboard-on-the-ground-and-run-away-screaming smile. "Don't worry. We're not full. I can get you in." She winked. Alexander felt weird. Like his face was on the surface of the sun, and his heartbeat was now his whole body instead of just his heart.

"You're really pretty, Mina," Theo said matter-of-factly. "Isn't she pretty, Alexander?"

Alexander's embarrassment felt like a tie that had been knotted too tight. Why would Theo just *say* that?

Fortunately, Mina saved Alexander once again by responding before he had to. "Thank you! That's very kind. What's your family's name so I can enter it?"

"The Sinister-Winterbottoms," Wil said.

"ABSOLUTELY NOT!" Mina shouted, her voice ringing through the lobby.

CHAPTER FIVE

Alexander withdrew into himself like a tortoise. He hated being shouted at. And his worries had been right: they *were* breaking some sort of rule by being here without parents! They couldn't check in or stay here. Back to the woods it was. Alexander didn't know whether it was possible for slugs to be poisonous— venomous? just regular old toxic?—but he was going to find out the hard way.

Theo's scowl blazed across her face. She also didn't like being shouted at, but unlike Alexander, it didn't make her hide. It made her immediately want to shout back. "Why can't we check in?" she demanded.

"Is there a problem?" Wil didn't seem concerned. Or if

she was, she was saving all her concern for Rodrigo. She looked at the screen like it was a fridge that had absolutely no leftover pizza at all.

"Yes! No, sorry, the problem's not you." Mina glared at the doors. Alexander and Theo turned. There was a flash of black velvet, a blur of movement behind a beam, but they didn't see what the problem was. Mina's smile popped back into place. "Where were we?" She glanced at the waiting group of people tapping their feet and clearing their throats and looking at their watches. Mina reached into the pocket of her trim pinstriped vest, and pulled out a pocket watch. "Oh *no*, we're behind schedule. The Count wants orientation to start now."

"The Count?" Theo asked.

"I just— There's so much to do, and only me to do it." There was a rush of humid air and Mina's glare came back. "Or at least, it *should* be only me." Theo and Alexander looked over their shoulders to see the pigtailed cowboy hat girl come in, cheerily leading the exhausted parents with the two sticky toddlers.

Why didn't Mina like that girl? Or did she not like sticky toddlers? The first was a mystery, but the second was pretty reasonable.

Mina's smile once again changed the subject. "Let

45

me check the computer to see if you have a reservation." Mina's computer was ancient, and the fan inside it whirred angrily while she typed something out on the clackety keyboard. "S-I-N-I-S— Oh, that's interesting." Mina frowned and tapped out some more letters. "It says there's a standing reservation for any Sinisters."

"And the hyphen is okay?" Alexander asked, not wanting to take any chances. At Fathoms of Fun, they hadn't read the entire liability waiver, and it had nearly ruined everything. He wasn't going to risk that happening again. "Because our mother was a Sinister, but then she married our father, so we're the Sinister-Winterbottoms."

"Our parents wanted to abuse as many letters of the alphabet as they could," Theo grumbled. Her full name was Theodora Artemisia Sinister-Winterbottom, and combined with Wilhelmina Camellia Sinister-Winterbottom and Alexander Hawthorne Juniper Rowan Alder Sinister-Winterbottom (since he was named last, their mother had thrown in every middle name she liked rather than choosing just one), they could fill nearly a whole page of writing with just their names alone.

Mina smiled. "I'm sure the addition of Winterbottom is not a problem. I'll give you the Harker Suite. It's a nice set of rooms. We usually put lawyers in there, but only when they've traveled a very long way. Let me just fill out the guest book, while you DON'T MOVE A MUSCLE!"

Once again Alexander flinched, Theo scowled, and Wil didn't even look up.

"Sorry. Not you. I just— Here." Mina shoved a large metal key at them. It had an elaborately engraved brass key chain attached that said *Harker Suite.* "Don't lose that, please. We lose so many keys, and important papers, and shoes. But only the left ones." Keeping her eyes on a corner near the ceiling where neither Theo nor Alexander could see anything, Mina scribbled *S-WINTERBOTTOM* in the guest book, along with the number 3 and *Harker Suite,* and then gave them a harried smile. "The orientation meeting is in the great ballroom, which is near the okay ballroom, which is across from the disappointing ballroom. If you'll please deposit your belongings in your room and then hurry to orientation, we can get started! Hello, welcome to the Sanguine Spa!" she said as the next family in line moved up, edging the Sinister-Winterbottoms out of the way.

Theo and Alexander dragged their suitcases to the side of the lobby, unsure where to go next.

"I'm taking my stuff to the room," Wil said, wandering

off, bumping into a suit of armor and not even apologizing to it before continuing on her way.

"Is it just me," Theo said, watching Wil with narrowed eyes, "or—"

"It's still not just you." Alexander sighed, worried. "And it's not just Rodrigo, either. There's something wrong with Wil. Ever since we've been with Aunt Saffronia, Wil never cackles in triumph, or shouts 'Get wrecked, big tech!' or even scrolls with a glazed expression. She's . . ."

"Up to something. Or in trouble." Theo understood both being up to something and being in trouble better than Alexander.

"So we'll keep an even bigger eye on her."

Theo opened her eyes as wide as she could, then crossed them. Alexander laughed, grateful at least that Theo was still on his side. They were a team.

A team that had to haul their suitcases to their room. They eyed the pile of luggage waiting in the corner of the lobby. No one else had taken theirs; they had just dumped them there for Mina to deal with. Mina, finally finished with check-in, stood in the middle of the mess, looking tired and lost.

"We could help her?" Alexander asked. Looking at Mina made him feel funny, and he didn't want to look at her, but he also didn't want to *not* be able to look at her. The reason why crushes are named crushes is because they literally crush your ability to think clearly: you like someone in a special way, but because you like them in a special way, being around them is *absolutely miserable*.

"Sure!" Theo didn't really care one way or another about looking at Mina, but helping deliver luggage meant they could see a lot of the hotel or spa or castle or whatever the building was, and she loved exploring. She also loved seeing other people's rooms and houses, always curious how they lived. Everyone was a mystery, and while she wasn't as interested in reading mysteries as Alexander was, she did like getting clues from looking at bedrooms and living rooms and inside fridges. You could tell a lot about a person by what toppings their leftover pizza had.

They crossed the lobby to Mina. "Can we help you?" Theo asked.

"Oh, that's so nice!" Mina said. "But I could never ask that of you."

"You didn't ask," Theo pointed out. "We offered."

Alexander wanted to say something, but his brain's connection to his tongue glitched as soon as Mina was in front of him.

"I suppose that's true," Mina said with a grateful smile.

"In that case, STOP THAT THIS INSTANT AND GO TO YOUR ROOM!"

Alexander's heart nearly stopped in response to Mina's command. "You don't want us to help?"

"What?" Mina blinked at them, which was when Alexander and Theo realized she *hadn't* been shouting at them at all. She had been looking straight up at the beams that crisscrossed the ceiling. They both looked up but didn't see anything other than shadows made deeper by the flickering candlelight of the chandelier.

"What was that about?" Theo asked.

Mina clapped her hands together, her tone bright and twinkling like the candles. "I do want your help, thank you! If you two can handle this huge trunk, I think I can get the rest. But the trunk is definitely a two-person job."

"Good thing we were born a two-person team!" Theo beamed.

Alexander wanted to say something clever, but it was hard to talk when he was looking at Mina. Partly because she was so pretty and partly because he was half-afraid she was about to yell again, and this time it might be about him or what he was doing. So he pushed their own suitcases against the wall and grabbed one side of the trunk.

"Oof," he said.

"Oof," Theo agreed. "What's in this thing?" She wanted to open it to see, but even she knew that was an invasion of privacy. Still, if they were carrying it, and she *accidentally* dropped it, and it fell and popped open, she would definitely look. No one could blame her then.

"I don't know. Quincy"—Mina wrinkled her nose when she said the name, as though she didn't like the taste of it in her mouth—"brought it with her, but it's not hers. The guest it belongs to hasn't checked in yet. If you could please take it down that hall, to the right, up one flight of stairs, and to the room at the end. You can leave it outside the door. Thank you! You two are really kind and helpful. It's nice to have someone actually help me for once." Mina's chin trembled and her large eyes pooled with tears, but before she could cry, her smile popped back into place. It seemed like it was as much a part of her uniform as the vest and the skirt and the name tag. She grabbed the nearest suitcases, getting back to work.

But not as much work as Theo and Alexander. Theo abandoned her secret plans to *accidentally* drop the trunk. Not because she wasn't curious anymore, but because dropping it would mean having to pick it up again, and she didn't want to do that.

They stopped to rest halfway down the hall. Unlike the polished wood floor of the lobby, the hall had plush deep red carpet. It was lined with chairs and benches. Normally Theo would think that was silly—hallways were for getting from one place to another, not for sitting and waiting—but she flopped onto a bench, glad to rest. There was a painting of an old-timey lady on the wall across from her.

"What do you think she ordered on her pizza?" Theo said, pointing.

Alexander sat next to her. He felt calmer now that they weren't near Mina, but he was still out of breath from lugging the luggage. The woman in the portrait had mounds and mounds of swirling golden curls on top of her head. Her black dress was embroidered with blood-red roses. She had one hand against her neck, and her face was turned to the side, her eyes downcast. But she was smiling like she had a secret.

Alexander thought the portrait looked like it was from a long time ago, before the glory days of pizza. But he played along. "Probably a lot of vegetables."

"Ugh. Yeah. Piles of arugula. Salad pizza," Theo said, wrinkling her nose. Why did people try to turn pizza into salads? Let a pizza be a pizza. No one ever got excited about wilted lettuce on top of their leftover fridge pizza. Salad pizza was almost as bad as putting meat and raisins into a pie. "What else do you think she was like?"

"I think she always cheated at Scrabble," he said. The twinkle in the woman's eyes, the twist of her smile, made him think she was up to something.

Theo nodded. "Yeah. But she cheated in, like, funny ways, so you couldn't even be mad. Like Dad when we play—"

"Literally anything," Alexander finished. Their dad was a notorious game cheater. And while Alexander was a notorious rule follower, even he laughed at the outrageous ways their dad came up with to cheat.

"*We made a bet I couldn't possibly lose,*" Theo whispered, repeating the tale of how their parents met. Their mother had told them so many times, gazing with a smile at their dad.

"*But you did,*" Alexander said, filling in his dad's part.

"*And in losing, I won.*" Theo sounded sad. This was the part in the story where their mother would grab their father and dance him around the kitchen, both of them laughing in a way that made Theo and Alexander feel like they were in on the joke, even though they didn't know what the joke was. But when their parents were dancing and laughing, everything was normal. Safe.

Alexander missed them, so much. So did Theo, but she didn't want to feel that way. It upset the hive of bees that lived in her chest. Scowling, she leaned forward, examining the painting more closely.

"What is she holding?" Theo asked. In the hand that wasn't against her neck, the woman had something small and fuzzy and brown.

"Maybe a very small dog, or a rat?" People in old paintings were always holding strange things. Alexander stood and moved closer. And then the painting *moved* as the fuzzy brown thing lifted its head and stared straight at them.

CHAPTER SIX

Alexander screamed. His scream startled Theo, so she screamed, too, which scared Alexander even more. They had never been the type of twins to dress alike, or even to be interested in the same things, but they definitely screamed well together. If there were an Olympic sport for synchronized screaming, they'd have earned at least the bronze. (Russia would win the gold, obviously, because they had all of Siberia to practice screaming in.)

"What's wrong?" Mina rushed down the hall toward them.

"The painting!" Alexander said. He pointed to where

the fuzzy brown part of the painting had moved and looked at him with beady black eyes, but . . .

There was nothing there. The woman's hand was empty.

"There was—it was—she was holding something, and it—it moved." Alexander couldn't believe his eyes. There had been something there, he was sure of it.

"The painting changed," Theo agreed. "She was holding a little brown fuzzy thing. Like a rat. Or a Chihuahua. Or a rat-Chihuahua hybrid. Which would be kind of pointless since they're basically the same breed already." Theo liked both rats and Chihuahuas, but they seemed to fill the same animal categories: small, furry, and terrifying when found in unexpected places.

Mina's face went pale with worry. But instead of looking at the painting, she looked straight up at the dark shadows of the ceiling. It was high, with the same crisscrossing support beams as the lobby. It was a ceiling that seemed to somehow soar overhead and press down menacingly at the same time. Usually ceilings are boring, but not in the Sanguine Spa.

"You two must be tired," Mina said, walking backward, eyes still up. Maybe she was the opposite of Wil, and always looked up instead of looking down. "I often see things when I'm tired. Shapes in the mist. Mysterious animals. Figures in the rafters. That sort of thing. Thanks again for your help with the trunk. You're almost there— keep going!"

She disappeared around a corner, still watching the ceiling.

"That was—" Theo started.

"Spooky?"

"That was—" Theo started again.

"Mildly suspicious?"

"That was aggravating," Theo finished. She always liked the word *aggravate*. It sounded like *aggressive* or *angry* or *grating*, all of which combined to make *aggravating*.

And Theo was definitely aggravated by the mysterious painting. She didn't want any surprises here, unless they were *Surprise! You get to rappel all day!* or *Surprise! Cake for every meal!* or *Surprise! Your parents are back with a perfectly good explanation for why they ditched you for the whole summer and left you with a hive of angry bees constantly buzzing in your chest!* types of surprises.

Theo leaned closer to the painting, glaring. "Aggravating, and spooky, and mildly suspicious. Spookily suspiciously aggravating. Is it just me, or is she smiling more now than she was before she made us scream?"

Alexander was pretty sure her face was the same, but then again, the painting had already moved, so who was he to say? All he knew was he no longer wanted to know what her favorite type of pizza was. After they ditched this luggage, he'd avoid this hallway.

"Come on," Alexander said, dragging the trunk. Theo pushed, and they wrangled it to the winding stairs at the end of the hallway. The stairs were stone, narrow, and spiraling, and not designed for the lugging of large trunks.

"No wonder Mina didn't want to do this," Theo said. They grunted and groaned, stopping often for breaks and to figure out how to unjam the trunk from where it kept getting jammed against the wall.

At last, they got it to the next floor. This hallway was empty, no plush carpet or chairs along the wall and, thankfully, no portraits or paintings. They passed a couple of doors before shoving the trunk in front of the door at the end, glad to be rid of it.

"I wonder if the person who owns the trunk is a driver? It says 'Van H.'" Theo pointed at a name etched into the lid. Unlike the wood of the lobby, which looked old but nice, the wood of the trunk looked old and menacing. Something about it—maybe the size, or the huge lock, or the various gouges that looked liked they could have been made by claws or knives—made it seem like a trunk they shouldn't want to open.

Of course, Theo often wanted to do things she shouldn't. But in this case, she didn't have any options. The lock was too big, and Alexander was right next to her. He'd never approve.

"'Van H.'?" Alexander read the letters, tracing them. He was grateful the trunk was in bad condition already. Doubtless they had dinged it on their way up, but hopefully whoever owned it wouldn't be able to tell. "Maybe. Doesn't seem like very practical luggage for a van driver, though."

"Could be an heirloom," Theo said. She loved that word even more than *aggravating*. When she was younger and her mother showed them some of their family heirlooms, Theo had assumed the word was *air-loom* and imagined her mother spinning stories of their family out of the air around them. Because that's what an heirloom is: an object that has stories already.

She clutched the timer she wore around her neck. It was a Black-Widow family heirloom that Edgar had given her, and she held on to it to try to distract herself. Thinking of her mom made Theo's angry bees stir to life.

Theo didn't miss her parents the same way Alexander

did. He got sad and worried when he thought about them. Theo got mad and annoyed. "Aggravating," she muttered to herself. "Come on. We're going to miss orientation."

"Since when do you like going to meetings?" Alexander followed her back down the hall.

"When those meetings include details on how I can swim and play games and hopefully rappel!" Theo skipped down the stairs, followed by Alexander, who inched down them.

"You don't think we'll *have* to do any of the activities, do you? They won't be mandatory?"

Theo laughed. "It's a vacation. You get to choose what you want to do, right? That's the whole point of a vacation."

"Someone should tell that to Aunt Saffronia," Alexander grumbled. Still, he *did* enjoy attending meetings. He liked learning all the rules, having every expectation neatly laid before him so he didn't accidentally do something wrong. Knowing exactly what was expected of him in a situation always comforted Alexander.

The twins had a problem, though. Mina had told them they were meeting in the great ballroom, but they didn't know where that was. They hurried back through the painting hall, Alexander deliberately not looking at the painting and Theo deliberately glaring and sticking her tongue out at it. But the lobby offered no clues as to where they should go.

Alexander grabbed their suitcases. Their mother had packed for them, and even though he was still hurt and sad about being dumped for the summer, he felt closer to his parents when he had the suitcases they packed.

"That way," Theo said confidently, because she'd rather be confidently wrong than tentatively right. She assumed the ballroom was on the main floor, and the hallway she picked was the widest. The first set of doors opened to a room filled with half-deflated balls of all varieties and a broken pump in the corner.

"Oh! We found the disappointing ballroom!" Theo said.

"That was . . . more literal than I was expecting."

"But we're on the right track!"

The next doors were thrown open to reveal a slightly dingy room. The windows looked out onto the drive, mostly asphalt in their view. It wasn't a bad room—there were a few sagging couches and a TV that was probably nice a decade or two ago. All in all . . . "It's okay," Alexander said.

"Right. The okay ballroom. So that means the next

room is . . . ," Theo said, grabbing a door and throwing it open. They were greeted with yawning darkness as wind shrieked toward them like a scream and Theo teetered on the edge of falling into the black void.

"You shouldn't be here," a voice like a ghostly whistle whispered.

CHAPTER
SEVEN

Alexander very much didn't want to scream again, so he had his mouth clamped shut. His face was nearly purple from holding it in.

Theo wasn't about to scream, but she did *not* like being startled, or opening doors into tunneled stairways of pitch-dark death, unless of course that was what she was trying to do. "Who's there?" Theo demanded.

The door slammed shut in their faces. Theo grabbed the knob, but it was locked.

"What was that?" Alexander asked, worried.

"A basement?" Theo asked, curious. She kept trying the doorknob. It was a metal face, with a keyhole in the middle, so it looked like the face was screaming as much as Alexander wanted to.

"Come on," Alexander said. He had no desire to open that door again or find out who had been whispering. And he was also worried they were going to be in trouble for arriving late to the orientation meeting.

Fortunately, they didn't have to search any longer. Around a bend in the hallway, the doors to the great ballroom were wide open. It really was a great ballroom, especially compared to the disappointing and okay ballrooms they had already seen. An elaborate forest scene decorated the ceiling. Combined with the exposed wood beams, it made the space feel like part of a forest. A forest filled with a lot of complaining people, but still, a pretty cool forest. The floor was polished wood covered with a deep green rug, the windows were stained glass with diamond patterns of different greens, and there was another chandelier hanging from the rafters like a weeping willow, dripping light from its branches.

Alexander peered up at the forest scene. He could almost swear there were eyes watching him from the darkest parts between ceiling beams and painted greenery. It was like the forest outside: beautiful but also menacing.

After a quick check to make sure there were no slugs stealthily stalking him, he kept his eyes firmly on the front of the room. Which was where his eyes wanted to be anyway, because Mina was there.

"Hello!" Mina said brightly. "If you could all take your seats?"

"Where should we take them?" one of the dads said, to a smattering of polite fake laughter, which is the only acceptable response to dad jokes. Dad jokes are never to be actually laughed at. "Ha, ha" can be said aloud, but even this will only encourage further dad jokery.

"Our dad would have said something funnier," Theo grumbled. "Not *very* much funnier, but a little funnier."

"I wish he were here to think of a better name for the spa castle. Caspa? Spastle?"

"Caspatle," Theo said, but they were interrupted by their sister bumping into them.

Wil somehow sensed that she had run into her siblings, as opposed to the strangers she had repeatedly walked right into. It was a matter of trial and error, really. If Wil bumped into enough people in a crowded room, eventually she would bump into the right people. "There you are. Did you twerps come to the room?"

"Yes, we were there the whole time," Theo said.

"We were spray-painting a new mural on the walls," Alexander added.

"We call it *An Ode to Bad Words*. Do you think they'll make us pay a fine?"

"I'm fine, too, thanks." Wil kept walking until she bumped into an empty chair. She sat down, and Theo and Alexander joined her, keeping their suitcases by their feet. Theo bounced in her chair, impatient to get this over with so they could get to the fun. Alexander sat perfectly straight and still in his chair, wishing he had a pad of paper and a pen to take notes. Maybe Mina would distribute a printed copy of everything she was about to say. He hoped so. While most people consider it a form of legal torture to have to sit and listen while someone reads the instructions *right in front of you* aloud, Alexander preferred it that way. Two ways to learn the rules at once!

"Thank you so much," Mina said, smiling sweetly. "I'd like to officially welcome you to the Sanguine Spa, and tell you DON'T EVEN THINK ABOUT IT!"

Everyone sat straighter in their chairs, mildly alarmed. Alexander's mind raced. What had he been thinking about that he wasn't supposed to?

But then he saw Mina was staring straight up at the

ceiling. He looked up, too, but couldn't tell if there was a moving shadow or if it was just the flickering light from the weeping willow chandelier. Alexander wished for some plain old lights that wouldn't cast creeping shadows in the rafters.

Theo scowled, folding her arms. This meeting was already taking too long.

"Ahem," Mina said, smiling, "I mean, don't even think about, um, not having a good time! Yes. That's it." The adults around her grumbled and squirmed in their seats. None of them were used to having to listen to a teenage girl. "To introduce our schedule, I've—"

A man swept into the room, much like a broom, only without cleaning anything. He wore a suit as dark as charcoal, with the red-satin-lined jacket flapping freely against his back like a cape. His hair was dark and slowly ebbing like the tide away from his forehead. His skin was pale, and his lips were unnervingly red, like he had just been drinking fruit punch and failed to wipe his mouth afterward.

"Oh," Mina said, and her smile wavered. "I thought—"

"Nonsense, sweet child. Thinking is for grown-ups." He smiled with what seemed like more teeth than normal people have. "No need for you to take charge. *I'm* in charge."

The adults in the room let out a sigh of relief, ready to listen now that a fellow grown-up was the one telling them what to do.

"Yes, Count," Mina said, still smiling, though it looked like it hurt her. She moved out of the way, and he took her place. And then the girl with pigtail braids and a cowboy hat came and stood at his side. "Quincy," Mina said, her voice dropping along with her smile.

"Mina," Quincy responded, her smile still bright.

"Welcome to the Sanguine Spa," the Count said, holding his arms wide. His jacket fell dramatically to the floor. "I think you'll all find your time here to be exactly what I need."

"What *you* need?" one of the mothers of the nesting-doll children asked, raising her hand timidly.

"Yes, what *you* need, of course! That's what I said. And what you need is to relax!" The Count's smile got even bigger, showing even more teeth.

"Yes, exactly!" the demanding dad with the bad dad jokes said, slamming a fist against his leg for emphasis. His son, next to him, nodded so fast his head was a blur.

"Is there a daily program of family activities?" the father of the two sticky toddlers asked. He was cleaning his hands with a diaper wipe, unaware that, at his feet, one of his toddlers was wiping his shoes with her applesauce.

The Count clapped his hands together. "All the adults will spend their days in the spa, being pampered and taken care of by my expert staff."

Theo looked around but saw only Mina. She hoped Mina wasn't the whole staff for an entire spa.

"What about our kids?" the other mother of the nesting-doll children asked.

"Don't worry about them," Quincy said with a cheery smile. She was idly twirling a length of rope. It shot out and looped around the nearest empty chair.

Theo raised her hand but spoke before the Count called on her. Unlike Alexander, she usually knew what the rules were but could only manage to follow one at a time. Raise your hand *and* wait to be called on before speaking was one step too many. "I don't want to go to the spa."

"Well, that's good," the Count said with a scowl, "because you're not allowed! Off-limits to children. Besides, you'll be much too busy with our children's activities, which are off-limits to adults."

"But when will we have family time?" the son of the bad-dad-jokes dad asked.

The Count laughed, tipping his head backward and exposing his long, long throat, where his Adam's apple bounced in merry delight to his fake laughter. It was even faker than the laughter reserved for bad dad jokes. "Ha! Ha! Ha!" he shouted. "Family time! You're here for a family vacation—a vacation *from* family, not a vacation *for* families! Isn't that right? Aren't you tired of being parents all day every day?"

The dad joke dad nodded as his son wilted in his chair. The parents of the two sticky toddlers seemed about ready to cry as they nodded. The nesting-doll mothers looked at each other across the vast distance of four children separating them, as though unsure how they should feel.

Alexander wondered . . . was this what their parents had done? Decided to take a vacation from them? He looked at Theo, but her face was like the impending storm outside, her fists clenched.

Theo was wondering the same thing, but instead of being sad, she was furious. All her bees were swarming in circles around her body, and she just wanted to get them out. She needed to move, and she needed to move *now*.

"So get on with it!" Theo shouted. "Let's go!"

The Count glared at her; then his smile slid back into place. "I like your attitude. Don't forget how eager you were. Now, parents, follow me to the spa while our children's program director gets the children situated in their room."

"Who's the children's program director?" one of the nesting-doll mothers asked.

"Me!" Quincy said, beaming.

"But . . . you're a child, too."

"Precisely," the Count said. "It's the children's program, not the adults' program! Off they go, and off we go."

"We aren't staying in the same room?" the sticky parents asked.

"Well, that would be no fun, would it? I need you perfectly relaxed."

Theo and Alexander shared a look. Or rather, passed two looks between them. Alexander was hurt, and Theo was angry. They always had fun with their parents. They were very fun children!

Weren't they?

The parents seemed to hesitate—some more than others—but then again, they *had* paid quite a bit of money for this vacation, and it had five stars on Gulp, so they had to trust that the system worked and that everyone would end up having fun. Wil stood up when the grown-ups did.

"Where are you going?" Alexander asked.

"Are you going to the spa?" Theo asked. "No kids allowed!"

"I'm basically an adult," Wil said.

"Says who?" demanded Theo.

Wil sighed, still tapping something into her phone. "I'm not going to some silly spa. But I'm not going to stay in a room with a bunch of kids I don't know. I don't like kids."

"We're kids," Alexander said, feeling the hurt welling inside his chest.

"No, you're twerps. *My* twerps." Wil finally looked up, flashing her brilliant smile as she mussed Alexander's hair in exactly the way he hated but let Wil do because he liked it when she paid attention to him. Her face softened, and she lowered the hand holding Rodrigo. "After the water park, you two deserve an actual vacation. This will be fun. You'll make friends. Look, those kids seem . . ." Wil glanced at the nesting-doll children, all sitting in a perfectly still line. "Well, that one seems . . ." She glanced at bad-dad-jokes junior, who was scowling, his face turning red with anger or frustration. "Well, those ones seem . . ." She glanced at the two sticky children, currently sitting under a chair, doing something unspeakable with a tube of diaper rash cream. "Well, she seems interesting," Wil said, sounding relieved at last to have noticed Quincy, who had lassoed twelve chairs and was slowly dragging them to the corner of the room, where they could be stacked.

"What will you be doing?" Alexander asked.

"Using the Wi-Fi." As though that explained everything, Wil walked out.

"Get moving," the Count hissed at Mina as he finished ushering the adults through a different set of doors than the entrance ones.

"I'm going to help the kids get settled."

"Well, then do it and come to the spa. There's no time to waste! I need them!"

"What?" Mina asked. "Why?"

The Count smiled, his dark eyes flashing with menace as he looked over the parents obediently shuffling out. "I mean, I need them to relax. . . ."

Alexander and Theo shared a troubled look, this time matching their expressions, like wearing the same outfit as your best friend. They didn't believe him for one second. What did he need them for, really?

CHAPTER
EIGHT

"What's behind that door?" Theo asked as Mina led the group past the locked mystery door.

"What? Nothing!" Mina smiled. "I mean, probably something. It is a door, after all. But this building is very old, and it's been locked for ages. No one knows where the key is. Come along."

Theo frowned at Alexander. He shrugged. He had no desire to have the door opened again.

Mina led them through the lobby, down the hallway past that terrible painting, and then down another hall, and another, until at last they reached a staircase. The stairs, much like the ones Alexander and Theo had dragged the trunk up, were windy and narrow. But with only their own suitcases, it was much easier. Most things in life are easier when you're not dragging a trunk. Imagine how difficult life must be for elephants, all the time.

At the top of the stairs was an entire floor of the castle made into a single, humongous room. Bunk beds lined up neatly along one wall like drawers to tuck the children in and put them away. The opposite wall had doors to individual bathrooms. In the center were game tables, pool tables, foosball tables, Ping-Pong tables, really any table that served a purpose other than dining. (Except for times tables, water tables, and tablespoons. None of those were visible.)

"Whoa," Alexander said.

"Whoa!" Theo agreed. Aunt Saffronia really *had* known what she was doing, sending them here. Between this awesome room, the activities outside, and friends to do things with, Theo was sure she'd be so busy that she wouldn't even notice her bees. It turned out spas weren't boring at all!

"Go ahead and pick out bunks," Mina said, a sentence every child hopes they'll hear someday. Alexander and Theo, despite being twins, had never had bunk beds. Their time had finally come.

They hurried over with the other kids, though there were so many bunks that everyone could get what they wanted. Theo, naturally, wanted a top bunk, and Alexander, naturally, wanted a bottom bunk. Theo was already planning a route on how to jump from bunk to bunk and make it across the entire room without touching the floor. And Alexander was already thinking how easy it would be to roll from a top bunk in your sleep, or to forget where you were and put your feet over the side to go to the bathroom in the middle of the night, only to be greeted with a plummet to pain and injury. Then you'd *still* need to go to the bathroom, and you'd be in pain, and really, is there any bigger betrayal than a bed that doesn't keep you safe?

Alexander patted the bottom bunk as he put his suitcase there, grateful for the bed's sensible proximity to the floor. Theo shoved her own suitcase against the wall.

"Isn't this awesome!" Quincy said, coming into the room behind Mina.

"I guess," bad-dad-jokes junior grumbled. "But we'll get to see our parents sometimes, right?"

"ABSOLUTELY NOT!" Mina shouted.

While the other kids went wide-eyed with shock that Mina was yelling at them, Theo and Alexander looked up.

Whatever Mina was shouting at, they couldn't tell. Alexander missed plain plaster ceilings very much. Anything could be up in that soaring ceiling, behind those beams and rafters. He retreated into his bunk bed, grateful to at least have the shield of another bed between himself and the ceiling.

Mina had already switched back to her sweet smile. "Now, we have a lot of activities planned for you, as I said." She paused and cleared her throat, glancing to the side at Quincy. "Don't we?"

"Oh, yes! Loads of activities." Quincy seemed much too young to have a job at a spa. She was the same age as Theo and Alexander, and they were definitely too young to have jobs, much less jobs putting them in charge of other kids.

"I'm going to win!" bad-dad-jokes junior shouted, puffing out his chest. "Whatever contests there are, or activities, or games! My dad said I need to be the best, and I'm going to, and he's going to be so proud!"

"That's nice," Mina said, smiling blandly at him.

It wasn't nice at all, Theo thought. She was good at nearly everything she tried to do—or at least, nearly everything she *wanted* to be good at, since she couldn't be bothered to care about being good at things like sitting still, or following directions, or golf—but her parents never put pressure on her. All they did was encourage.

Well, that was all they did when they were around. Her bees buzzed to angry life as she looked at this kid who had his father *here*, when hers was who knows where. Something burned in Theo's heart. She was going to beat that boy at *every single task*, no matter what.

"Now, let's do introductions!" Mina chirped. "I'm Mina. This is Quincy," Mina said, but the way her mouth tightened into a line made it sound like she was unhappy about it. "She'll be in charge of children's programming this week."

"I will!" Quincy had a nice twang to her voice, like she was from Texas. "I'm from Texas," she confirmed, which is a thing that people from Texas will always tell you because it's a legal requirement of living there. It's exactly the opposite of being from Delaware. In Delaware, you're sworn to secrecy that you live there so people will continue to wonder whether or not Delaware is, in fact, a real place.

(It is. But it's nothing like what you're imagining. And don't let the Delawarians know you're imagining Delaware. There's a reason it rhymes with "Beware.")

"I'm Ren!" bad-dad-jokes junior shouted. "I'll be your helper, Mina! Your assistant! I'll run the games!"

Theo glared, her fists clenching. If Ren was running the games, he could cheat. Theo suspected he definitely would. And not in a funny, playful way like their dad, but in an annoying little *cheater, cheater, pumpkin eater* sort of way.

"Thank you, that's very kind," Mina said. "But I'm afraid Quincy is in charge here. Besides, Alexander is already my assistant." She flashed Alexander a smile, and his heart did something weird and uncomfortable. All his blood went right to his face, turning him bright red under his freckles. "Theo, too," Mina continued. "They've been my assistants since they volunteered to help me with some hard tasks earlier."

Theo tried not to smile smugly at Ren. It was difficult. Some kids just radiate obnoxiousness. Sort of like a boiled egg. Put one boiled egg in the fridge, and it didn't matter what else was in there when you opened the door, leftover pizza included: you were hit with a wave of THERE IS A BOILED EGG HERE smell, undeniable and unavoidable.

Ren was like that. As soon as he opened his mouth,

the other kids knew he wasn't going to be fun. It was undeniable and unavoidable.

It also wasn't really his fault, and Alexander wanted to give him a lot of chances. Sometimes, when someone is obnoxious and you *treat* them like they're obnoxious, it just makes the obnoxiousness worse, like a scared animal spreading out fur or feathers to make itself seem bigger.

Theo, however, had no such patience. Her mother would be disappointed in her, but her mother wasn't here, so. She could be as unfriendly as she wanted without a gentle voice encouraging her to look for ways to make room for different people. Theo already felt a little bad about it, though. That was another feeling she didn't want buzzing around in her, so she squashed it.

The four nesting-doll children lined up in descending height order.

"Oh!" Mina said. "You're Josephine and Josie's children. Your names are?"

"Joseph," the tallest said.

"Joey," the second tallest said.

"Jojo," the third tallest said.

"Let me guess," Theo said. "Jo?"

The fourth tallest—technically the smallest, though

fourth tallest sounded more impressive—frowned as though the suggestion made no sense. "No, I'm Eris."

Alexander and Theo shared a confused look. "Maybe they ran out of *Jo-* names?" Alexander whispered.

"Or they got bored," Theo said. She certainly would have. "I feel better about our names now, though. At least they aren't just the same recycled name."

"Yeah. Then we would have had Wilhelmina, Willow, and William."

"I'd make a good Willow," Theo said, jutting out her chin. But she was wrong. Theo was exactly the right name for her, and any other name would have fit like clothes made for someone else.

"You'd make a good Oak," Alexander said.

"I'd make a good Pine."

"You'd make a good—"

"STOP THAT AT ONCE!" Mina shouted.

Alexander felt a weird prickling on the back of his neck. He whirled around and could have sworn there was a flash of dark movement between the bunk beds and the wall, but it was gone before he could be sure it was there.

"Stop what?" Quincy asked, scratching her head under her hat, as puzzled as the rest of them.

"Now," Mina said, as though she hadn't just inexplicably shouted, "I'm very excited! You're the first visitors we've had since—" She stopped, her smile freezing in place like a painting. But a painting that took a *very* long time, so the person being painted had to sit, smiling, until their cheeks trembled with pain and exhaustion. "Well, you're the first group we've had in some time. It's good to have the spa full again. For our first activity, we're going to—"

"I'll take it from here," the Count said, sweeping into the room like an industrial broom pushing away everything it met. In this case, pushing away Mina so he could stand in front of her. Quincy moved to his side as he gazed over the children with a critical eye. "We're going to have a scavenger hunt."

"YES!" Alexander shouted, surprising everyone, including himself.

CHAPTER NINE

Alexander blushed, embarrassed by his excited outburst. If he were a strip of paint samples, his color would be Please Stop Looking at Me Red. He cleared his throat, then said in a much softer voice, "I like scavenger hunts." He'd thought they were on one in the Fathoms of Fun, but it turned out to be just a regular mystery, not a fun game mystery.

Theo, while not as outwardly pumped as Alexander, was also excited. She darted a smug glance at Ren. He didn't stand a chance. Thanks to their yearly family scavenger hunt practice, Team Sinister-Winterbottom Twins was going to absolutely dominate this competition.

"Good," the Count said, but he didn't seem pleased.

He glared at the children in front of him. Much in the same way he swept into the room, he looked as though he would prefer to sweep them right out and into the trash. The Count was the type of person who *never* had leftover pizza in his fridge. He let out a long sigh. "Very well. Get to it, then. No time to waste."

"Where's the first clue?" Alexander asked.

"Clue?" The Count frowned.

"You know. The starting clue. The one that begins the hunt so we can follow the first clue to the next clue."

"Oh," the Count said. "There are no clues. If I had clues, I wouldn't need you, would I?"

"Then how will we know what we're looking for?" Theo asked, confused.

"Or when we've found it?" Alexander added.

The Count put one long-fingered hand over his face, his voice low and despairing. "It's almost as though you don't understand how important this is. That everything depends on it!"

"I really don't understand, though," Theo said.

Alexander's excitement was deflating like a balloon, making a sad squeaking sound in his soul. "This doesn't seem like a scavenger hunt."

"Well, it *is* a scavenger hunt because I said so and I'm a grown-up. Now! You're wasting time! Get looking!"

Quincy cleared her throat. "Actually, Count, we decided to put a hold on the scavenger hunt. *Remember?*" She glanced over at where Mina was glaring at them. Quincy's voice dropped to a whisper, but because she was from Texas, even her whispers were very big. "We decided it could wait? Until there weren't so many *people* to know what we were looking for?"

The Count scowled. "Very well." He turned and swept back out like the world's worst broom—one that came into a room and messed everything up instead of leaving it tidy and welcoming.

"Why don't you all settle in with some games?" Quincy said.

"I'm going to win!" Ren screamed, racing over and hovering near the game tables to see who would challenge him. Eris and the Js followed in a line. The two sticky toddlers, whom everyone seemed to have forgotten about, were painting the wall with a horrifyingly questionable brown substance.

"This week is going to be great!" Quincy spun her ropes, then whipped them out, neatly catching the ankles of the two sticky toddlers. They had been halfway inside a bathroom, reaching for the toilet-bowl water. Quincy carefully pulled them out, then did something fast and incredible with the rope that flipped the two small children in the air and deposited them safely and neatly in the center of a beanbag chair. They both squealed with delight.

Theo watched with deep admiration. "Can you teach me to do that?" She had never before realized what an essential life skill lassoing was.

"Sure! But later. We've got some great activities today," Quincy said, gathering her rope back in. "The ropes course, of course. Then the lap pool, and meditation, and mani-pedis, and sand art, and the sauna. I have it all planned."

Mina's hands were fluttering like birds that had been trapped inside, unsure where to go. "I— Well, that isn't what *I* had planned."

"Did you want to do the scavenger hunt?" Alexander asked. He didn't actually want to do a scavenger hunt with no rules or clues. Just *calling* something a scavenger hunt didn't *make* it one.

"It's not up to me," Mina said, eyes filling with tears.

"Okay," Alexander said hurriedly, not wanting her to

cry. "But if you like scavenger hunts, we could make one together? I'm good at writing clues!"

Mina sat sadly on the edge of a bunk. "No. The last thing I want is anyone looking so hard they find— Well, anyway, the Count is in charge. I can't contradict him. And he has his own help." Mina darted a pained look at where Quincy was keeping the two sticky toddlers busy by jumping rope, then sighed. "It wasn't always like this."

"What was it like when it wasn't like this?" Theo asked.

"When my parents were here, it was wonderful. We had ever so much fun. And I didn't have to worry that—" The light in her eyes dimmed, and her chin trembled. "But they're gone now, and the Count is in charge. He's been very generous to let me stay here and to give me a job. Well, several jobs. Well, all the jobs, really, except the ones I used to do." Mina stood with a sigh. "Speaking of which, I have to give seven massages, run a meditation circle, administer the Count's special essential oil relaxation blend, prep the mani-pedis for you, and make dinner for everyone. I'd better get going. I wish I could help you all have fun. Do try to, even without me."

Alexander nodded as fast as he could, not wanting Mina to worry about them. If she wanted him to have fun, he absolutely would not let her down. It was very, very important to him to make Mina happy.

Theo had already stopped thinking about Mina, watching Quincy instead. "How did you get a job here? Is the Count your dad or your uncle or something?"

"No, my uncle's not here yet," Quincy said. Something about her voice snapped tight and closed, like the loop of the rope she sent sailing behind herself. It flew around the post of a bunk bed before snagging the two sticky toddlers as they were about to fall off a top bunk. They dangled by their ankles, giggling. Quincy slowly released the slack of the rope and lowered them safely to the floor.

"Where did you learn to do that?" Theo asked, wildly impressed.

"My mom taught me. It's vital in our family's line of work."

"So you work with horses?"

"No, I'm allergic."

"Cows, then?" Alexander asked.

"Nope, allergic to them, too. And to grass, and to hay, and to dust. About the only thing I'm not allergic to is rope." She flicked one of her lassos up, and it spelled out QUINCY in midair. Then she shouted a yip and whipped her rope through the air so it made a loud cracking noise.

"Okay! Time to get moving, friends!" But Ren ignored her, playing foosball against himself and somehow still losing. Eris and the Js were very absorbed with arranging the pool balls in descending numerical order.

"Can't they stay here and play those games?" Theo was antsy to get to the ropes course and actually preferred it if all the kids didn't join them. More time for her!

"No," Quincy said, her tone serious. "It's my job to keep you all busy, and if they stay here, they might decide they want their parents. That's not allowed." She widened the loop of her lasso, then flung it out so it snagged Ren, Joseph, Joey, Jojo, and Eris. "Come on," she said, tugging.

Alexander and Theo hurried to the door lest they, too, be quite literally lassoed into participating. Apparently, activities were *not* optional.

CHAPTER
TEN

Theo and Alexander followed Quincy down the stairs and out into the hall. She had released the older children from her lasso, but the allergy-prone cowgirl still led the two sticky toddlers. It was much like herding sheep, if sheep were kids who were really too young to be on their own without constant, vigilant parental supervision, and instead of wool they had lots of fluff and fuzz and string and dust stuck to them on account of how sticky they were.

"Okay!" Quincy declared, leading them to the disappointing ballroom. Theo kicked one of the flat balls, and it thunked sadly against the wall before slumping to the floor. "Here's a sign-up sheet! You can choose which activities you want to do, though some are mandatory."

"Ropes course!" Theo shouted.

"That's my favorite!" Quincy said, surprising exactly no one. "We can head over there as a group!"

"Can I . . . do something else?" Alexander asked, meek but hopeful. He didn't want to do the ropes course, and he didn't want to watch Theo do it and be nervous the whole time, and he also didn't want to somehow end up in charge of the two sticky toddlers while everyone else had fun. Being responsible for his own safety was often overwhelming; he had no desire to be responsible for the safety of small children.

"Sure! Take your pick, as long as you stay busy." Quincy slid the clipboard over to him.

Alexander appreciated Quincy's color-coded organization on the sheet. He wouldn't have expected it of her. "Oh! Can I take kitchen duty?" He felt his heart pick up speed, but not out of fear or worry for once.

"Sure!" Quincy wrote him in and then went to help the other kids figure out their schedules.

"Kitchen duty?" Theo asked, incredulous. "What is that, even?"

"Meal planning and preparation!"

"So . . . you're providing free labor. For the spa we're paying to be at."

Alexander shrugged. He'd always imagined being on *The Magnificent English Confectionary Challenge*, though he'd never admit it. "At least this way I can make sure everything is prepared with rigid safety standards."

"Except you don't have a food handler's permit." Theo raised an eyebrow teasingly.

Alexander's stomach dropped. It was true. He *should* have a food handler's permit. In all fairness, he knew everything they taught in the course, having re-created it one rainy afternoon with his dad just for fun. But he didn't technically have it.

"I was kidding!" Theo said quickly, seeing Alexander's face fall with disappointment. "I'm sure it doesn't matter!"

"Quincy," Alexander said, "I don't have a food handler's permit."

"Well, you can get one online, and we'll just print it off."

"Really?" Alexander felt like his soul was filled with sunshine. Everything was looking up as the twins separated to their various thrilling activities.

Theo flung herself along ropes and balanced on

boards, even helping Eris and the Js navigate—which was challenging, since they always insisted on doing everything in a line one after the other. But Theo loved the challenge (and she loved that Ren couldn't keep up with her). Her heart raced as she dangled above two paths, deciding which to navigate, instinctively picking the best one. Which, for Theo, was the most difficult one.

Alexander, meanwhile, sat at the ancient lobby computer, dutifully taking notes and answering multiple-choice questions. Though their tasks were very different, Alexander's heart also raced as he dangled above two true-or-false questions, deciding which was correct. And his delighted *yip* of triumph as he passed the test was just as loud and joyous as Theo's when she finished the course in record time.

Alexander hurried to the kitchen, printed certification clutched in his hand. He carefully taped it on the wall so anyone who wanted to inspect it could, then surveyed his new kingdom.

The cupboards were nicely stocked. There were the basics but also a few odd things like jars of Marshmallow Fluff and a whole shelf of maraschino cherries soaking in vivid violet-red liquid.

Always a young man with excellent priorities, he made

cookie dough first and put it in the fridge for later. Then he looked at the meal schedule. All the old options— braised boar, roasted stag, and (*yuck*) blood sausage—had been aggressively crossed out and replaced with options like cruelty-free vegetable hash, cleansing green juice, and something called "replenishing infusion." Which didn't sound like food at all.

But he had a job to do. He dutifully followed the directions and added various vials of liquid and packets of powder to blenders full of fruits and vegetables. In his head, a narrator was detailing all his actions, and the judges were looking on in shocked approval. They'd never imagined such a young person being so proficient at following directions!

Once Alexander had finished blending, he portioned the smoothies, then stocked them all in the freezer. This was Mina's job, and Alexander was saving her a lot of work. He blushed just imagining her saying thank you.

No time for that. The imaginary judges were watching! Soon it would be dinner. This was his moment to truly wow them.

He opted for classics: caprese salad, which he liked because it was actually just cheese, tomatoes, and basil with a nice vinaigrette dressing; spaghetti with red sauce;

and garlic bread. The kitchen was absolutely packed with garlic. Garlic cloves, garlic salt, garlic butter. Whoever stocked it really liked garlic. Like, a *lot*.

Alexander whistled to himself, mashing garlic. As soon as the fumes hit him, he backed away, his eyes watering. There was an odd hissing noise from one of the cupboards. Frowning, he opened it. There was a flash of movement that filled him with dread—rodents!—but when he flung it open all the way, it was empty, just one jar of maraschino cherries sitting there. The lid was partway off. Had it been that way before?

No time to worry about it. He had judges to impress.

Outside on the ropes course, impressed with herself, Theo laughed and looked at her timer. "That makes me in the lead, Quincy next, followed by Joseph, Joey, Jojo, Eris, and . . . Ren." She tried not to smile too big at that.

Ren huffed, sweating and red-faced. "Not fair. I have an injury, and I didn't wear the right shoes, and if I were the one timing, I bet I'd win!"

Theo tucked her timer back under her shirt. "Let's race through the maze, then."

"No!" Quincy said. "The maze is off-limits. We don't go in there." She glanced at it, a worried twist to her mouth.

"But we came in that way," Theo said. "It wasn't too bad. And it was obvious someone's been in there. There were footprints."

Quincy's eyes widened. "What . . . kind of footprints?"

Theo frowned. "Kid footprints?"

Quincy let out a relieved laugh. "Well, that can't be. I was the only kid here before your arrival. I tried to do it but ended up lost in there for two hours. It's impossible to get through. Even the Count can't! Here, race me!"

Quincy tossed the lasso holding the two sticky toddlers to Eris, then took off like a shot. Theo chased her, all her bees lulled into quiet happiness. Theo was so busy, so active, she didn't have time to worry or to think or to feel anything other than the exhilaration of movement and competition and climbing and learning to lasso, just like Alexander was so busy, so occupied, he didn't have time to worry or to think or to stress out about anything other than adjusting the oven temperature and wondering what altitude they were at and how that would affect his cookies.

The ropes course was hers, and the kitchen was his, and the darkness beneath them was someone else's entirely.

CHAPTER ELEVEN

"Hey!" Theo, out of breath, grimy, and happy, leaned into the kitchen. "Come on. It's mandatory mani-pedi time. Everyone's already headed over there."

"Oh, good! I need you." Alexander, calm, perfectly clean, and happy, readied another baking sheet. "I'm using the kitchen timer for the cookies, but I need one for the garlic bread. It can't burn. Two minutes, tops."

"On it," Theo said. There were too many steps and too many things to keep track of in baking for her, but she could do this. She started her timer and pressed her face against the oven glass, watching as the tops of the bread went from pale to slightly darker to perfectly golden.

"Time!" she shouted, and moved out of the way as an

oven-mitted Alexander removed the bread. While Theo washed her hands and face, Alexander pulled the last batch of cookies from the other oven and set them to cool on the counter.

"Okay," he said. "Mandatory manicures. So I guess you could say they're . . . mani-datories."

"If you want to get pedi-antic about it." She grinned, and they walked into the lobby. "Is it weird that I'm excited? I've never done this before."

"Me neither." Their father would occasionally go get a mani-pedi as a treat, but their mother said her feet were secrets best left to the darkness. Actually, now that Alexander thought about it, he'd literally never seen her without at least socks on.

Off the lobby was a short hallway. It led to double doors with golden letters above that said *SANGUINE SPA: FOR WHEN YOU ARE DRAINED.*

Theo pushed confidently through the doors. Alexander followed far more timidly. "I thought children weren't allowed in the spa?" he said.

"We're not, except for the mani-pedi area specially set aside for us. Quincy told me to find her as soon as I had you." But that was a problem now that they were inside.

Because there was no obvious indication where Quincy and the other children had gone.

The waiting room of the spa was what adults would look at and think, *Ahhhhh.* Long leather couches, plush green carpet, smooth white walls, a fountain in the corner.

Theo looked at it and thought, *Yawwwwn.* It seemed awfully boring to her. It could just as well have been the waiting room for a nice doctor's office or a particularly swanky dentist. There was a check-in desk with no one behind it, and two frosted glass doors leading into the rest of the spa.

"Maybe we should wait here for Quincy to come get us," Alexander said, not wanting to risk getting in trouble. The dentist-like setting already had him worried he might have a cavity, even though he took meticulous care of his teeth and, besides, spas weren't about teeth. Were they? The fountain in the corner did look like it was made of very sharp canine teeth (one could even say fangs), pointing downward with water flowing off them.

Alexander had never been in a spa before, and new places and experiences always made him extra nervous. Usually his mother was with him, to reassure him and to model how he was supposed to act. But without her here, he had no one to copy. He certainly wasn't going to copy Theo, who was currently leaning way over the desk, practically on top of it.

"Oh!" Theo yelped, backing up. A head full of dark braids appeared from behind the desk.

"Wil? Is this the activity you chose?" Alexander asked, puzzled. Maybe she had opted to help in the spa, like he did in the kitchen.

Wil held a finger to her lips. "I was never here." She scurried out into the hall, the doors closing behind her.

Theo went around the desk. One drawer was partially ajar. She pulled it open and found a bunch of folders with people's names. Had Wil been looking at them? If so, why? Theo shrugged it off. Odds were, Wil was just on the hunt for the strongest Wi-Fi signal.

Theo was bored with waiting. There was only one set of doors other than the entrance. Theo strode forward and opened them.

"What the *what?*" she whispered. Alexander hurried to look at what she saw, but also had no words for it.

He had expected an all-white room, much like the waiting room. Instead, the space looked more like a cave. Several steps led downward. There were no windows, only several heavy brass doors set deep into the thick stone walls. A few sconces burned, giving dim, smoky light. The rocks of the walls were undecorated save leering, fanged faces glaring down from the deepest shadows near the curved stone ceiling.

But the design of the room wasn't the strangest part.

Lying on small tables lined up in neat rows like a mortuary, draped in black robes with black satin sashes over their eyes, were all the parents. None of them moved or seemed aware of anything at all. There was a humming white noise drowning out any of the small noises living people make, so that Theo and Alexander couldn't even be sure the parents were breathing. Next to each occupied table was a tray. And on each tray were several vials of dark red liquid.

"Why do they have towels over their necks?" Theo whispered, pointing. Each throat was draped with a small scarlet cloth, hiding the skin there.

"What is this place?" Alexander whispered.

"You shouldn't be here," a voice answered behind them as hands came down on their shoulders with viselike strength.

Theo and Alexander were yanked back into the lobby of the spa. The Count glared down at them as he folded his arms. "I told you, no children in the spa. They don't want you here. They're trying to relax. They need to be drained."

"Drained of what?" Alexander asked, more than a little alarmed. He couldn't get the image of those little red vials out of his mind. They were too small for drinks, or lotion, or anything else he could think of that someone might want in a spa.

The Count cleared his throat, his eyes darting away. Theo could always tell when adults were lying because they had such a specific way of doing it. The Count was literally looking around the room for whatever lie he was about to tell them. "Drained of their stress, of course."

Theo and Alexander shared a dubious look. Maybe this was what people did in spas, though. Maybe all spas were cave-like, barely lit, with people lying around like corpses. It didn't seem like a fun thing to do, but adults did lots of things for fun that absolutely baffled Theo and Alexander. Not their own parents, who had cool hobbies like building battle robots and translating ancient books, but they had friends whose parents did things like garden, or collect tiny glasses from restaurants, or nap. Was there anything more boring than sleeping when you didn't have to?

"We're here for our mani-datories," Theo said.

"Your *what?*" One side of the Count's unnervingly red lips rose like a question mark.

"There you are!"

Alexander and Theo turned to see Quincy. She had opened a door set into the wall, so white and plain they had missed it.

"Come on!" she said. "I have the two sticky toddlers tied to the chairs, but they'll get out soon, and I can't leave the polish unattended!"

The Count pushed them toward Quincy. Alexander got one last look over his shoulder at the mysterious cave-like room before the Count closed the door, sealing the parents away.

"What are they doing in there?" Alexander asked, but Quincy and Theo had already gone into the mani-datory room, leaving him alone.

There was a hint of a breeze on the back of his neck. Alexander slapped his hand over it, feeling goose bumps rise as he could swear he heard a hint of a giggle. But when he spun around, he was alone.

"Wait for me!" he shouted, never in his life more eager to get his nails painted.

CHAPTER
TWELVE

The Sinister-Winterbottom twins, it turned out, did not like getting manicures and pedicures.

It was nothing against the nail polish itself. Theo had been thrilled by the selection, choosing traffic-cone orange for her fingernails and toxic-spill green for her toenails. Alexander had opted against getting a manicure, knowing how often he needed to wash his hands to follow the food safety protocols he had just been certified for. But he did choose a soothing teal for his toenails.

Neither of them, however, had accounted for how long it would take to dry. They followed Quincy down the hallway and through the lobby, carrying their shoes, shuffling awkwardly in foam flip-flops.

"I can't use my hands or run?" Theo grumbled. "This is a nightmare."

Alexander never wore sandals, and he finally understood what his mom meant by *feet should be secrets*. He wanted his feet to be a secret again. Being essentially barefoot against the cold gray stone floor left him feeling oddly vulnerable. But he kept looking up rather than down.

"Is there something wrong with your neck?" Theo asked.

Alexander stopped craning it up. "Do you feel like you're being watched?" he asked.

"No, I feel like I— Argh! There, see, I messed up the polish. I knew I would." Now it looked like a car had crashed right through her traffic cone of a fingernail. "How can anyone stay still long enough for this stuff to dry?"

"Straight to the cafetorium!" Quincy shouted, guiding the procession of children. Joseph, Joey, and Jojo had all opted for beige nail polish, while Eris brought up the rear with black. Quincy had done the two sticky toddlers' nails in Day-Glo yellow with a glow-in-the-dark topcoat, "just in case." Alexander wondered what case that was.

Ren had refused to get his nails painted, saying his father wouldn't want him to, so instead he had slouched, scowling, arms folded and feet getting more and more wrinkled in the foot bath. He had ended up looking like he had bleached raisins for toes. Bleached toe raisins were, categorically, the only thing worse than actual raisins.

Quincy led them all to the cafetorium, a large room connected to the kitchen. Like its name suggested, the cafetorium was a multipurpose space. The floor was polished wood and the walls were stone, but there were basketball hoops descending from the ceiling and a stage on the far side. Between them and the stage were several folding tables and chairs.

Alexander paused by the entrance door. There was a sheet of paper tacked there to sign up for a talent show. He froze with momentary panic: he didn't have a talent to perform! They couldn't make him go onstage! But then he looked closer. The date at the top was a year ago, from last summer. Among names he didn't recognize were several, oddly, that he did. The Black-Widows, for one. That was Edgar and his dads. And beneath them, Mina and family.

What must it be like to be back in this space without her parents, with all those happy memories hanging around the rafters, upside down now with grief and loss?

The schedule under the sign-ups looked different, too. Something called Batminton tournaments—surely that was a typo, since the game was badminton—plus guided walks through the woods, maze races, and—

"Catacomb Laser Tag?" Theo exclaimed, reading over Alexander's shoulder. "When can we do that?"

"We can't," Quincy said, ushering in the two sticky toddlers. "We lost them."

"The laser tag guns?" Alexander asked.

"No, the catacombs."

"How—how do you lose catacombs?" Theo asked. She knew from reading about Paris that catacombs were extensive, subterranean tunnels. Usually used to house bones. Alexander didn't know that, and Theo didn't tell him, because she was a kind sister who understood that a lot of things that lit her brain up with "COOL!" lit Alexander's brain up with "FEAR!"

Quincy shrugged and went back to handling the toddlers. "Come on, you gremlins. Take a seat."

Also on the sign-up sheet were lots of spa options—salt scrubs and saunas and something called hot rock massages, which sounded painful because who wanted to be massaged by a hot rock?—but it seemed like there were mostly things to do as families, together.

Why had that changed?

"Hello!" Mina said brightly, greeting them.

Alexander turned and wrapped his arms around her in a hug. "I'm so sorry about your parents," he said. Unlike Theo, who didn't know how to feel her *own* feelings, Alexander always felt everything, deeply, even when the feelings weren't his own. He had such a good imagination from always envisioning a million different ways things could go wrong that he could also imagine what it would be to feel things he had never felt. Right now, he was feeling what it must be like for Mina to run the first season of the spa without her parents. So much the same, but nothing the same at all.

Mina put her arms around Alexander and rested her head on the top of his. "Thank you," she said, her voice soft, catching just a bit like she wanted to cry but didn't have time for it. "And do I have you to thank for all the meal prep in the kitchen?"

Alexander nodded, letting go of Mina and stepping back. If his face was a nail polish color, it would be Please Let Me Disappear pink.

"Can we help more? With serving dinner, I mean."

"Yes, please," Mina said. "Would you two go get the trays out of the kitchen and bring them in while I finish setting the tables? I meant to have it all ready by now, but I've been stuck in the spa."

"Doing what?" Alexander asked, hoping she would give him answers.

"DON'T THINK I DON'T SEE EXACTLY WHAT YOU'RE DOING!"

Alexander flinched. "I'm sorry. I know it's off-limits and we shouldn't have seen, but we did, and I can't stop thinking about it, and—"

Mina blinked rapidly, looking back down at Alexander. Theo turned to try to see what Mina had been focusing on, but the ceiling was so high, she couldn't make out any details up there.

"Oh, no, sorry," Mina hurried. "Of course you're curious. To answer your question, honestly, I'm not even sure what we're doing in the spa. It's all so different since the Count took over. But that's okay. Sometimes change is good!" Mina forced a smile and hurried over to finish setting the tables.

Theo and Alexander went into the kitchen. He had left everything that needed to be warm in warming drawers, and everything that needed to be cold in the fridge, and everything that needed to be room temperature in the room. Everything was exactly right.

Except . . .

"There were more cookies," he said.

"Mina must have taken them," Theo said, because if she were Mina, she definitely would have.

But Alexander didn't think Mina would leave a trail of crumbs along the counter, ending underneath the cupboard with the maraschino cherries that hadn't been properly closed. He opened the cupboard, half expecting something brown and fuzzy to appear, and so was relieved to find only a jar of Marshmallow Fluff.

But . . . no cherries.

"Huh," he said, but there was no time to dwell on it. He grabbed trays of food—only one for each hand, whereas Theo balanced two on each arm and one on her head. They set them on the tables.

Quincy straightened from where she had been whispering something to Ren. He opened his mouth, but she put a finger over her own mouth and winked.

Ren was quickly distracted by the food offerings. "I wanted chicken nuggets," he said, scowling.

"When are the adults joining us?" Alexander asked,

wanting to question them about the spa and to ask Wil if she'd gone in there at all.

"Oh, they're not," Quincy said. "Total separation. Now eat up! We have a fun after-dinner activity planned!"

Theo didn't need telling twice. Mina finished setting the table, setting pitchers of dark red fruit punch in front of them. Maybe that was where the Count got his lip coloring. Alexander eyed the pitchers warily, not wanting fruit-punch mouth himself.

"Did you like the cookies?" he asked her, hopeful.

"Oh, I haven't touched them! But I'm looking forward to one at the end of the day. I've got to get the infusions to the spa now." Mina rushed away.

"Who ate cookies, then?" Alexander asked.

"Anyone with any sense," Theo said. "You make good cookies."

"Yes," a voice whispered. Alexander whirled around, but he didn't see anyone.

"Look closer," he muttered to himself.

"What?" Quincy asked.

Alexander shook his head, surprised she had been listening. "It's what our aunt told us when she dropped us off. She said we needed to be able to look closer. And I can't help but feel like there's something . . . weird here."

"No!" Quincy blurted out. "No. There's nothing weird here. You just need more to do with your time! You need to be busier. I can keep you busier! I *will* keep you busier."

"I—"

"If you want to look for something," she said, leaning closer, eyes so wide and bright they were almost feverish, "both of you can do the scavenger hunt. It's important, too. It'll really help us—I mean me—out. And I have a clue for you."

"Yes!" Alexander shouted once more, his voice ringing through the cafetorium, shocking everyone there.

CHAPTER

THIRTEEN

"Sorry," Alexander said, awkwardly clearing his throat. Everyone went back to their meal. "What's the first clue?"

Quincy twirled her pasta around on her fork, looking down at the noodles as if considering whether or not she could make them into lassos. "Well, there's only one clue, really. And you have to keep it a secret. Both the clue and the fact that you're looking. You can only tell the Count or me if you find something."

"Or Mina?" Alexander asked, hopeful.

"No!" Quincy's fork scraped against the plate with a terrible screeching noise. "No. Don't tell Mina. She already has so much work. We don't want to add to it, right?"

"Right," Theo said, without hesitating.

". . . Right," Alexander said, hesitating. He really wanted Mina to be part of this.

"Okay, here's your clue: it's flat and rectangular."

Alexander's face fell along with his hopes. He liked Quincy a lot, so he didn't have the heart to tell her that was a terrible clue. And if it was the only clue, this wasn't really a scavenger hunt at all. He forced a smile and gave her a thumbs-up. "Got it."

"Maybe we should write it down," Theo grumbled. Alexander elbowed her, and she faked a smile, too. "Just kidding. Got it." After all, Quincy was doing a lot, too, running their whole program. The least Theo could do was humor the other girl. Plus, it was in Theo's best interest to keep Quincy happy. A happy Quincy was a lassoing Quincy, and Theo really did want to learn some rope tricks. Quincy had given her a length of rope, but it wasn't as easy as the cowgirl made it look.

"Remember," Quincy said. "Keep it a secret. And . . . it's important. Really important. I trust you two to help me with this."

She went back to managing the two sticky toddlers

and also fielding complaints from Ren. Theo made a spaghetti sandwich out of everything, then shoveled it into her face as fast as she could. "Come on," she said around a mouth full of marinara. "I think I solved it."

"Already?" Alexander asked, disappointed. He missed the cemetery, looking at all the old names and dates, working as a team with Theo and Wil. Knowing their parents were at the end.

"Yup." Theo tapped her fork impatiently while Alexander finished his dinner; then, being responsible children even when they were on a mission, they cleared their plates and washed their dishes. "Can you make churros tomorrow?" Theo asked, grabbing a cookie.

Alexander eyed the cookies warily. There were definitely more missing. None of the kids had come into the kitchen. And Mina had said she wouldn't eat any until after she was done.

"Churros?" Theo prodded.

Alexander shook his head. "They don't have the right equipment."

Theo sighed, taking her second and then third cookies. "I suppose these are an okay substitute."

"Guess what the spa's only cookie recipe called for?"

"No," Theo shuddered. "Don't say it."

"Raisins!"

Theo stuck her tongue out, grimacing. "I'm so glad you have sense."

"And taste."

"And a strong moral compass telling you to make the right decision in the face of evil."

"And also our parents' cookie recipes memorized."

"Let's go," Theo growled, her bees swarming up at the reminder of their parents. She led the way out of the kitchen.

Alexander quickly realized where they were heading, and began dragging his teal-toenailed feet. But when they got to the long hallway with the blood-red carpet and the painting with the horrible disappearing fuzzy brown thing, there was a different portrait in the place of the woman.

"Are we in the right spot?" Theo was confused because she was *never* confused about direction. She was very good at navigation, at reading maps, and at figuring out how to get from point A to point B in both the fastest and most interesting ways. And she had definitely led them to the right hall. But now it was the wrong painting.

In place of the mysterious woman's portrait, there was a man's. He was sallow, with a high forehead and a nose that told many stories, most of which were about his nose being broken. He held a cane with a silver head that looked like a wolf head on a sleek dragon-snake body. But the part they couldn't look away from was his eyes, staring down imperiously. They had been painted so they glowed with an almost-red light.

"I think I like this one even less." Alexander said.

Theo stuck her tongue out at the man. She didn't appreciate how he was looking at her, like he knew more than she did. She hated not knowing what other people knew. It was a big reason why Alexander read mysteries, but Theo read nonfiction.

"Who changed the painting?" Alexander asked. "Maybe that's part of the hunt. Or a clue."

"Maybe." Theo could have sworn she heard a faint whisper of laughter above them and looked up, trying to pierce the dark beams crisscrossing the ceiling. "Alexander," she said, "is it just me, or do you feel like you're being—"

"Theo!" Alexander said, reaching out and grabbing her hand. "Is it just me, or is the painting . . . moving?"

CHAPTER

FOURTEEN

When someone says, "Is it just me?" sometimes they're hoping it isn't just them, and the other person will reassure them that they aren't alone in their intense hatred of raisins. But sometimes when someone says, "Is it just me?" they're really, truly hoping it *is* just them, and the other person will reassure them that their idea that a painting is *breathing* is just a product of their wildly anxious imagination.

Unfortunately, this time it really wasn't just Alexander. There was a hint of movement as the painting pushed ever so slightly outward, then retreated. In and out, like slow, secret breaths.

"I miss the mysteriously disappearing fuzzy brown

part of the other painting," Alexander said, taking a step backward. "At least it had the decency to disappear after scaring us."

Theo swallowed hard. She was brave. Extraordinarily, sometimes recklessly brave, but staring at a painting that might be alive was a different kind of scary than, say, a giant waterslide. "Well, this is definitely flat and rectangular and noteworthy. We should go tell Quincy."

Theo turned and sprinted down the hall, but she was brought to an abrupt halt as she ran right into the Count. He loomed over her, scowling. "What are you doing?" he demanded. "Shouldn't you be with the other children?"

"We're doing the scavenger hunt!" she said. Alexander appeared behind her, having the sense not to run and therefore having the good fortune not to literally run right into the Count. Theo rubbed her shoulder. Running into him really had been like being smacked by a broom handle. "And we found something flat and rectangular, like Quincy said."

"Flat and . . . ah. Yes." The Count's eyes glowed with feverish eagerness. His fingers twitched in anticipation. "Show me," he commanded. The Count followed them to the painting.

Alexander braced himself to once again face the

creepy man. "What the *what?*" he exclaimed. Because where the breathing painting had been, there was now a portrait of two girls. And not just any girls. Mina stared out from the frame, fixing her dark eyes right on him. Mina had her hand on a little girl's shoulder as though holding her in place. That girl had blond hair floating around her head like a halo, and intensely black eyes. Her mouth was closed tightly with a hint of a smile, and she leaned toward the edge of the frame as though she were about to escape.

"This?" the Count sneered. "Just another blood painting?"

"Blood painting?" Theo asked.

"The Blood girls," the Count said, gesturing at the painting. "Lucy and Mina Blood."

"Mina's last name is Blood?" Theodora Sinister-Winterbottom asked, incredulous.

"It's Welsh," the Count said, as though that explained everything. "I think the portrait of their parents is around here somewhere. Unless that disappeared, too. Things around here have a habit of disappearing. Paintings. Keys. Parents. Little sisters." He stared at the portrait.

"Mina has a sister?"

"She isn't here anymore. This is nothing," the Count

said with a weary sigh. "Keep looking. Everything depends on your success. . . ."

Theo glared at his back as he walked way. "It's just a silly hunt," she muttered. "Not even a good one."

Alexander couldn't worry about why the Count was so invested in the scavenger hunt. He was too puzzled, looking at the new portrait. What happened to Lucy? Who was changing the pictures? And why?

Or . . . were the pictures changing themselves, and if so, how?

"Well, that was a bust," Theo grumbled. "What else do we know that's flat and rectangular?"

"Pieces of paper," Alexander said, tugging Theo's arm and leading her out of that horrible hallway.

"There were all those files in the spa, but surely they don't want us to go through them. What else?"

"What's lost?"

"The catacombs!" Theo said, excited.

"But those aren't flat or rectangular."

"True." Theo scowled. She really wanted to find them.

"What if—what if what Quincy wants us to look for is also what Aunt Saffronia wanted us to find?" Alexander stopped. He had led them to a specific door without thinking, without even meaning to. "Doors are flat and rectangular." He reached out and touched the horrible face-shaped doorknob.

Theo tugged and twisted it. "Still locked. And why would they need us to find this door? It's right here."

"True. Wouldn't make sense to have us look for a door unless—" Alexander stopped, eyes going wide.

"Unless it was a door where no door should be."

"A door in a rock in the middle of the woods beyond a maze."

"Alexander!" Theo crowed. "You genius." Then she paused. "But we're not supposed to go in the maze. Quincy said so."

"Oh." Alexander's spirits sank. He had been so sure he was on to something. "Did she say why?"

"No. And actually, it was before she told us about the scavenger hunt. So she probably meant it was off-limits as a group activity, but since this is just our special activity—you and me—I can't imagine it would be a problem."

"Are you sure? We should ask permission," he said.

"We should!" Theo laughed. Which Alexander took to mean she was going to, and which she meant as they really ought to but she wasn't going to because she didn't want to and didn't think she should have to. The maze was part of the spa, and they were guests of the spa, after all.

But it was already evening outside. And while Theo wanted to time herself going through the maze and see how quickly she could do it, she didn't really want to start out in the dark. It would mess up her speed.

"We have active meditation time in the morning. Whatever that is, it sounds boring," Theo said. "So we'll go then."

Alexander was about to double-check that Theo was definitely going to get permission, when they were interrupted by a crackling announcement over hidden speakers.

"Bedtime," the Count said, his voice all around them. "Mandatory bedtime. All children are to report to the bunk room for their safety."

"For our *safety?*" Alexander asked.

"There you are!" Quincy skipped into the hall, lasso twirling. "Come on! It's bedtime! We have to be in the bunk room! Hurry, hurry!" She waved her lasso, and Alexander and Theo rushed to get ahead of it. The hallways and stairs passed in a blur, and then they were in the room with all the other children. Quincy was behind them, locking the door.

123

"We're locked in?" Alexander asked, aghast.

"Or everyone else is locked out," Theo said with a shrug. She really needed to learn lockpicking. She added it to her list of new skills to acquire, alongside lassoing and rappelling.

"Just for safety!" Quincy said, tucking the key into her hat.

"What does that mean?" Alexander didn't like the way they kept saying *safety*. He very much liked the concept of safety, but if a door was locked for safety, that meant leaving it unlocked was dangerous.

"It's a big building, lots of stairs, very dark at night. And you'd be unsupervised if you went out alone. What kind of adult would leave you unsupervised?"

"Aunt Saffronia," Theo said. It was true. Which meant, by extension, their parents would, too, since they were the ones who had left them under the unsupervised supervision of Aunt Saffronia.

"Well, the Count isn't that type of adult," Quincy said.

Alexander made a small, dubious noise.

"I know he seems . . . odd. But I promise, he has your best interests at heart. All our best interests, really. Things are going to be okay. Better than okay. They're going to be normal." Quincy beamed at them, and Alexander smiled back. That was all he wanted—a normal summer, with his parents.

"Okay!" Quincy shouted. "Pajamas on, teeth brushed, beds occupied!" Some of the other kids groaned in disagreement.

It wasn't fair to Quincy that she was only twelve and had to be in charge of other kids. While Theo had never had any interest in babysitting, she did have an interest in helping out friends. She whipped out her timer and held it up in the air. "Whoever can be totally ready for bed and under the covers in three minutes gets—" Theo paused, unsure what to offer.

"A deconstructed s'more for breakfast!" Alexander had had the idea earlier in the day but had wanted to experiment with it before adding it to the menu. He expected lots of demands to explain what a deconstructed s'more was, and why they should want one, but he underestimated how much a bunch of children would be motivated by the idea of a dessert eaten at an inappropriate time.

"I didn't know they could move this fast," Quincy said. Then she slapped her forehead. "I've got to get ready, too. I want one of those!"

Theo and Alexander laughed at the mad rush they'd

created, then joined it. And sure enough, at the three-minute mark, every single child, including the two sticky toddlers, were safely in bed.

The day full of navigating ropes courses and/or preparing food courses and individually being pulled aside and told they were getting a clue to the scavenger hunt and must keep it secret had thoroughly worn out every single kid. Which meant every single pair of eyes fluttered shut in sleep within minutes.

Except, of course, for the pair of eyes looming in the rafters above, unseen but seeing all.

CHAPTER
FIFTEEN

Alexander was in a bed that wasn't his own. The room around him was expanding impossibly large into the black void of night, and he knew if he opened his mouth to scream, it wouldn't work. There was someone sitting at the foot of his bed, where no someone should be.

"Shhh," the someone said. The someone was digging through his suitcase.

It was enough annoyance to cut through the overwhelming terror. Alexander sat up. The someone on the end of his bed was hard to see in the darkness, but she had a halo of blond hair around her face.

"Please don't," Alexander said quietly. "That's my

suitcase. My mom packed it specially for me. Did you need something?" He leaned forward, and the little blond creature backed up with a hiss, pressing herself against the wall.

Alexander reached into the open suitcase and was surprised to find his fingers closing around an old yo-yo his dad had carved for him. He hadn't played with it in years. What was it doing in his suitcase? He looked down at it, remembering how hard he had worked to learn tricks with it, how carefully he had detangled the string when those tricks didn't work.

"Here," he said softly, holding it out to the creature. She reached out one tiny hand, fingernails as black as the night around them, and snatched it away, then crawled straight up the wall.

Alexander was glad he knew he was dreaming; otherwise, he probably would have screamed. He carefully lay back down, closing his eyes and willing himself to have a more pleasant dream.

Theo couldn't remember climbing out of her bunk or leaving the room. She found herself on the cold stone stairs, following a flash of blond hair and an echoing giggle.

"I'm dreaming," Theo said. She was pretty sure she was dreaming because she was out of the room and the room was locked. Though maybe in her dream she knew how to pick locks. She'd like that. She'd like even more to be able to pick them in real life, though.

She continued down the stairs, everything fuzzy and wrapped in confusion. The painting in the hall was gone. Now it was just a hole, with flapping bits of darkness going in and out.

Theo blinked, her feet moving almost of their own accord. When she opened her eyes again, she was on the edge of that doorway down into nothingness. The one that was locked. The one that no one had the key to.

The one that was open in front of her.

"Do you want to play a game?" a voice whispered.

"Sure," Theo said, because even in her creepiest dreams she was competitive, and she wanted to win this game.

The voice had moved. It was right next to her ear, tickling her skin. "What's my sixth-favorite animal?"

Theo frowned. "How am I supposed to know that without any clues? I'm going back to bed." She turned and walked, and the next thing she knew she was opening her eyes. It was morning.

Light streamed in from the windows in the bunk room. Everyone around her was still tucked in and asleep. Quincy was snoring lightly, snuggled up to one of her ropes.

"What a stupid dream," Theo muttered to herself. *Sixth-favorite animal?* That was the worst game ever.

She rolled onto her side and realized two things at once: she was in a different bunk than she had gone to sleep in, and the formerly locked door to the bunk room was wide open.

CHAPTER
SIXTEEN

"We're going to make breakfast!" Theo shouted as soon as Alexander was out of the bathroom, ready for the day. She grabbed his hand and tugged him from the bunk room.

He was still puzzled about why his suitcase was out on his bed, open, when he woke up. He had looked through it, but he didn't think anything was missing. Except, of course, a yo-yo that he was pretty sure wasn't in there to begin with. After all, why would his mom—who somehow always knew exactly what to pack in a suitcase, almost like magic—have packed a toy he hadn't played with in years?

Alexander let Theo tug him to the kitchen. He

assembled the breakfast plates for everyone. Even though "breakfast" was the wrong word. He put a little Marshmallow Fluff into a bowl in the center of the plate, then carefully surrounded it with graham crackers and chocolate chips for dipping, and then made enough chocolate milk for all the kids.

"Deconstructed s'mores! We're all going to get cavities," he said sadly.

"We'll brush our teeth twice as good tonight," Theo said happily, around a mouth full of graham cracker crumbs and marshmallow mushiness. "I started sleepwalking again," she said.

"What?" Alexander asked around his own much smaller bite.

Theo shrugged. "Weird dreams. No biggie. Now, let's go to the maze before they come down here and we have to ditch them!" She rushed out of the kitchen, and Alexander dutifully followed.

He assumed Theo had asked Quincy's permission while he was in the bathroom. At least she had given him enough time to make breakfast. "Oh!" he said as they rushed through the hall. "I didn't make anything for the adults!"

"They have that smoothie stuff, right?"

Alexander nodded. "Yeah. Lots of weird powders and liquids added. Seems kind of awful, drinking every meal. Wouldn't you get bored?"

"Lots of animals only drink and never eat." Theo frowned. Animals. "What would you say your sixth-favorite animal is?"

"Sixth?" Alexander had never thought to rank them. But before he could answer, they were in the lobby, and much to their surprise, they found something. Or rather, some*one*.

Wil was at the front desk, eyes glued to a different screen than normal as she tapped furiously on the ancient computer keyboard. "But why?" she whispered. "Which Sinisters made the reservation?"

"Wil?" Theo said.

Wil jumped like she'd been caught with her hand in the cookie jar. Though the Sinister-Winterbottom family didn't even own a cookie jar since cookies never lasted long enough to make it from the baking tray to anywhere other than someone's tummy. This was because their parents were good people who understood that cookies required chocolate chips, never raisins.

Never. Raisins.

"Oh, hey, twerps," Wil said, her voice deliberately casual and calm. "Where are you off to so early?" But as soon as she asked, she had Rodrigo back in hand.

"Burying a body," Theo said.

"But it's okay because it's not a human body," Alexander added.

"Alien," Theo said. "But it's okay because it's not a dead body."

"Nope, still alive! Makes burying a bigger challenge."

"That's nice. Have fun." Wil wandered away.

"What do you think she was up to?" Alexander asked.

"Maybe trying to get a better Wi-Fi signal. Or looking up the reservation to see how much this is costing, or something grown-up and responsible like that. Or maybe she was hacking the whole system to bring it crashing down and overthrow the spa. Who knows."

"Let's check in with her when we get back." Alexander had said they'd keep a better eye on her, but they were so busy.

They opened the huge brass doors and were greeted with a wall of humidity. It was like a giant was standing right there, breathing on them. The morning sky was a grumble of gray. It promised rain in much the same way you might know what's for dinner when you walk in the kitchen and smell the horrible dirt scent of beets. It's not there yet, but it's coming, and you can't get away from it.

Alexander followed Theo's stomping gait around to the back of the hotel. They froze. The parents were all sitting beneath draping black sunshades, only their feet in the pool, each with a smoothie in hand, sunglasses on, and headphones in.

"Don't mind us," Theo said, but not a single one of them so much as moved.

"It's like they're . . . hypnotized?" Alexander said. He really, really didn't understand spas.

"Come on, before the rain!" Theo hurried toward the hedge maze, but the first warm fat drops of rain were already falling. "Should we go back?" She glared up at the clouds, personally offended that they chose *this* moment to let go of their heavy burden. It always worked like that. The clouds had had all night to rain, but no. They waited until she wanted to be outside. Just like when it didn't rain during spelling tests at school but started pouring during recess. If Theo could have punched clouds, she would have, quite often.

Alexander didn't want to get rained on, but he also didn't want to walk past all the creepy, vacant parents again. Besides, they were already wet. "No, let's just get it done."

"Okay." Theo started her timer, glad it was old and weird but still waterproof. She really loved this timer. It even had her initials on the bottom, like it was always meant to be hers.

They entered the maze. This time, there were no footprints they could see. Theo regretted not finding a high-up caspatle window to study the maze from above. By the time they made it out of the other end, it had been thirty-two minutes exactly, and the rain was picking up.

Theo eyed the forest entrance to the maze, already thinking through her path back. "No wonder Quincy doesn't want us doing the maze. Can you imagine being stuck in there with the two sticky toddlers, or worse, the one unsticky Ren?"

"Didn't," Alexander corrected her.

"What?"

"*Didn't* want us doing the maze. Past tense. You said doesn't, which makes it sound like it's present tense, which means Quincy still doesn't want us doing the maze, which means you didn't get permission. You did get permission, right?"

Theo winced. "Well . . . I mean, it's silly! She's our same age! It's not like she's our babysitter."

"Theo!" Alexander glared. "You said you'd get permission!"

"No, I agreed that we *should* get permission." Theo wrinkled her nose, feeling guilty. But it was a feeling she wasn't good at, so instead, the bees flared to life and she buzzed angrily. "Besides, it's part of the spa, and we're guests of the spa, so what does it matter?"

Alexander folded his arms. "It matters to me, and you know it."

"Come on," Theo said.

"We should go back."

"Then go by yourself! I'm checking out the door." Theo took off down the trail, feeling sorry and grouchy and soggy, a very bad combination indeed. Her feet squelched through the mud, which was already thick like overcooked pudding, sucking so hard at their shoes that each step threatened to remove them.

Alexander, not wanting to be alone and knowing he

needed Theo to get back through the maze, was forced to follow. Everything was miserable. Somehow the rain was making the air even more humid. The rain was wet and warm, the air was wet and warm, it was all wet and warm and uncomfortable.

Theo and Alexander walked in angry silence, both annoyed with the other and annoyed that the other was annoyed when really *they* were the only one with any right to be annoyed.

They arrived at the boulders over the cliff face. Theo walked up to the door in the rock and tugged, but it didn't budge. "Locked," she grumbled. "And I couldn't pick it even if I knew how to. There's a keypad."

Alexander frowned down at the keypad. Normally he respected locked doors, but a keypad required a code, which was like a puzzle, which belonged in a scavenger hunt. And the keypad was arguably flat and rectangular, too. So maybe figuring out how to unlock it was part of the game?

He had read enough mystery novels to know he couldn't try random numbers and hope to get lucky. But if he gathered enough information, he might be able to guess what the Sanguine Spa would use as a code.

Theo, however, was perfectly willing to try random

numbers and hope to get lucky. She started punching them in.

"WHAT ARE YOU DOING?" Mina shouted. Alexander and Theo looked around to see what Mina was looking up at. That's when they realized that Mina was yelling . . . at them.

CHAPTER
SEVENTEEN

"We were just looking," Theo said, feeling defensive. She couldn't believe that this time, Mina was actually yelling at them.

"No one is supposed to be out here!" Mina glanced over her shoulder, watching the pathway behind them like she expected someone or something to come down it. Alexander looked that way, too, tense with apprehension. Maybe the Count was coming. Maybe the man from the portrait was coming. Maybe the slugs were coming.

But the path remained empty. Mina let out a sigh of relief, then shook her head, her wet hair clinging to her shoulders. "I'm sorry. I shouldn't have yelled. But don't tell anyone about this place, okay? *Anyone.*" She emphasized that last word.

"Why?" Theo asked. Theo was mostly willing to follow rules and instructions but not arbitrarily. She liked the word *arbitrary*. It was spiky and complicated, a barbed word to mean something with no meaning. If she was going to follow a rule, there had to be a reason. Theo didn't believe in arbitrary obedience.

Alexander did. He already felt bad about going through the maze when they weren't supposed to, and now he felt terrible for being where they weren't supposed to be, and even worse for upsetting Mina, and even most worst for getting yelled at by someone he liked. That *never* happened to him. He dragged a shoe through the mud, keeping his eyes on the ground, furious and embarrassed and upset. This was all Theo's fault.

"Well, you can't be out here because . . . it's not safe," Mina said after a pause. "There's a cliff right there."

"Oh, yeah, we know," Theo said with a dismissive wave. "Wil almost wandered off it earlier."

"She did?" Mina looked appropriately horrified.

"Yeah, she does that sometimes. But we keep an eye on her."

Mina smiled at that. "I'll bet you do. She's lucky to have you. We all need a sibling to look out for us."

"Did you look out for Lucy?" Theo asked.

Alexander's eyes got big, and he tried to telepathically scream *SHUT UP* at Theo, but they never had been the psychically connected type of twins.

"Yes," Mina said. Her eyes had gotten big and sad again. "It's the most important job I've ever had. And the most difficult. And the most dangerous."

"Dangerous?" Alexander asked, swallowing. "What . . . what happened to her?"

"It doesn't matter. She's gone. And that's what's important." Her voice got very serious and very firm. "Lucy is gone. Do you understand?"

They both nodded. Alexander didn't know whether that just meant Lucy wasn't here at the spa anymore, or Lucy wasn't here on the earth anymore, and he didn't want to ask and risk upsetting Mina any more than they already had.

"Right. Good. Okay, let's get back." Mina put her arms around their shoulders and turned them around, steering them toward the maze. "And please don't mention that silly door to anyone. We wouldn't want the other children coming out here and getting lost. It's not safe outside the spa. So this is our secret, okay?"

Alexander and Theo looked at each other. They sure were gathering a lot of secrets, but very few answers. And why was everything here so unsafe?

"Okay," Alexander said before Theo could ask why or argue. He was still mad at her, and if Mina needed this to be a secret, then it would be a secret.

Mina led them through the maze. She did it in exactly seven minutes—Theo timed it—which meant Mina must have done it many, many times. She never took a single wrong turn. Once they were inside the caspatle, Mina directed them to find the other children, then disappeared toward the spa. She had so much work to do, and now she was behind.

Which made Alexander feel even worse, but which made Theo wonder. If Mina was so busy, why was she out in the woods looking around *right* when they were out there? It was almost like she had followed them. Which meant she had seen them go out there. Which meant they were being watched.

"Hmm," Theo said.

"What?" Alexander asked, still upset. He loved rules.

He liked wrapping himself up in them like a sweater, all cozy and protective, keeping him safe from getting in trouble. Theo was like a snag, unraveling that sweater.

"Nothing," Theo said. "Or something. But nothing for now. Maybe something later. Come on. Let's go to Wil's room and get towels." Now that they were inside the chill stone interior of the caspatle, it was cold to be this wet. Wil's room was closer than the bunk bed chamber, and they could check on her.

They hadn't actually been to Wil's room yet. It took them a few hallways and several sets of stairs, but eventually they found the Harker Suite. For once in this confusing caspatle, a door was unlocked when they wanted it to be. They let themselves in.

"Hey, Wil!" Theo called. "It's us, a couple of robbers! We're here to take your shoes! But only the left ones because we're evil robbers, dedicated to a life of being really obnoxious!" Theo looked at Alexander, waiting for him to add onto the silliness, but he folded his arms, silent and still mad at her.

It didn't matter. Theo was performing for no one. The room was empty, with Wil nowhere to be seen. There was a sofa with clawed feet, a desk with clawed feet, and a big four-poster bed complete with gauzy curtains. And also clawed feet. All the feet had actual claws, too, sharp and wicked-looking. The four spindly posts of the bed were carved to curve gently upward, like the fountain downstairs. Almost like you were laying to go to sleep in the jaws of some massive creature. Every piece of wood in the caspatle had eyes or teeth or claws.

"This is . . . interesting," Theo said, touching one of the bed curtains.

A bang startled them as one of the lead-paned windows blew open. Alexander rushed to close it before water got in. But as he swung the window shut, something on the window frame moved. He looked up, straight into the beady black eyes of the small brown thing from the painting.

CHAPTER
EIGHTEEN

"The painting creature is here!" Alexander shouted, pointing to the fuzzy brown thing hanging from the top of the window frame. The fuzzy brown thing just blinked at him, fuzzily. And also brownly.

Theo rushed to Alexander's side. Theo had many interests, including geometry, history, world records, the various quality of different bubble gum brands, waterslide friction and timing, how much ice cream could be consumed in one sitting before a headache set in, and churros. And now lockpicking and lassoing. But she also really liked animals, and thus, unlike Alexander, she knew exactly what she was looking at.

It was a bit like a fuzzy brown burrito, tightly wrapped, with a head, ears, and eyes sticking out, and a funny squashed nose. And, if it unwrapped, webbed wings. And, if it opened its mouth, sharp little fangs.

"That," she said, slowly reaching up and closing the window all the way so the diamond panes of glass were between them and the creature that was definitely not a painting come to life, "is a bat. Actually, I think it's a . . . vampire bat."

"A *vampire* bat?" Alexander repeated. "So you're telling me that's a bat that lives on blood? By drinking blood? Like a—"

"Vampire," Theo said, nodding.

Alexander had never been so grateful for windows and glass in his life. He still took several steps backward, just in case. "Does it strike you as odd," Alexander said, who didn't know nearly as much about animals as Theo did but who had read a lot more books with supernatural spooks in them than she had, "that we are at a spa run by a man named the Count, and he separated all the grown-ups from the kids, and this place is built like a castle, and there are vampire bats hanging around—literally?" He gestured at the window frame.

"Everything here strikes me as odd," Theo said with

a shrug, but she agreed. There was definitely something going on at the Sanguine Spa *other* than relaxation.

"Didn't he say he was . . . draining the parents?" Alexander remembered those vials of red liquid next to the unmoving bodies of the grown-ups. Before, the vials had been puzzling. Now, though, they were scary.

"Let's not jump to conclusions." Theo loved jumping—on beds, off walls, into pools of water—but she was feeling scared, and she didn't like it. She didn't want to be scared. So she wasn't going to be. "Here's what we'll do," she said, because the bees inside her did better when she had a plan she could focus on. "We'll go find Quincy. She works here. She'll know more."

Alexander folded his arms stubbornly. He was still mad at Theo. "You didn't think Quincy was old enough to ask permission from, but now she's old enough to advise us about vampires?"

Theo threw her arms in the air. "I said I was sorry!"

"I don't think you did!"

"Well, I was sorry! Sort of!" She stormed into the hallway and down the stairs, but she was so mad at Alexander for being mad at her that she accidentally went the wrong way. Which made her even madder because she never went the wrong way. They ended up in the long hallway with the stupid changing painting. Theo stomped down it, with Alexander on her heels.

He was mad at her, too, and scared, but scared won out. He didn't want to be alone in a vampire-bat-filled caspatle. When Theo stopped abruptly, Alexander bumped right into her.

"Look," she said.

The painting had changed again. In this one, Mina and her sister, Lucy, were both younger, and behind them stood people Alexander assumed were their parents. Which was unfortunate because they were the scary people from the other portraits—the woman who held the bat that crawled out of the painting to hang around outside Wil's room and the man with the repeatedly broken nose and the cane. But in this painting, they didn't look like they had a secret. They looked . . . happy. Their hands were on Mina's and Lucy's shoulders. But less like they were holding them back and more like they were proud of their daughters.

Everyone in the painting looked happy, actually. It made Alexander realize that Mina's constant sweet smile was also a constant sad smile.

"Look at the background," Theo said.

Alexander had been so focused on the faces that he

hadn't looked closer at what else was going on in the painting. "Are they in a cave?" he asked.

Along the top of the painting hung stalactites, not unlike the ones in the Cold, Unknowable Sea back at Fathoms of Fun. But unlike the one in the Cold, Unknowable Sea, these ones weren't dripping with water. If anything, they looked fuzzy. Like if Alexander made a loud noise, dozens of tiny brown fuzzy flying vampires might flap right out of the painting.

Alexander backed up until his legs bumped into the bench. "I really hate this hallway."

"And is it just me, or is it even colder than the rest of the caspatle?" Theo rubbed her arms. "Also, this reminds me of the dream I had last night about Lucy. When I was sleepwalking."

"Wait, you had a dream about Lucy last night?" Alexander sat on the bench, afraid to take his eyes off the painting lest it change again. "I think I did, too."

"What was your dream?"

"She was getting into my suitcase. I gave her my old yo-yo, and she crawled up the wall. What was yours?"

"I followed her down this hall. But there was no painting. Just a hole in the wall with a bunch of bats flying out.

And then she tried to get me to go through that locked door down the stairs, but I went back to bed instead."

"Why would we both dream about a girl we'd only seen in a painting?" Alexander asked.

"This morning, the bunk room door was unlocked. And it couldn't have been Quincy. She was still asleep."

"My suitcase was out on my bed and open. I know I wouldn't have left it open." Alexander never left his things out. His room was always tidy.

"Do you think— What if—"

"What are you two doing here?"

Theo and Alexander whipped around to find the Count looming in the entrance to the hallway.

"Looking!" Alexander squeaked, unable to stop himself from looking right at the Count's red, red lips.

"And what do you expect to find in a hallway?" The Count's red, red lips pursed tighter.

"What do we expect to find *anywhere*?" Alexander asked, desperate. He was scared and frustrated, and this was the worst scavenger hunt ever. But for the first time he was actually glad that his parents weren't here. If they were, they'd be in the spa, and he didn't want anyone he loved going near that place. "What are we looking for?"

"Yeah," Theo grouched. "This isn't even fun anymore."

The Count's eyebrows shifted, and he looked . . . worried. "You think you're here to have *fun?* If only it were that simple." He gazed down the hallway, drawing the collar of his draping suit jacket higher around his neck. "Everything depends on finding what was lost."

"Like Aunt Saffronia," Alexander whispered, elbowing Theo. "She wanted us to look closer."

"But—" Theo started, only to be cut off by the Count holding up a single hand with long, long fingers, each ending in a fingernail that was just a little too long for comfort.

"Do you hear that?" He looked up toward the ceiling, narrowing his eyes. Then he rushed away, leaving them alone once more.

"Weird," Alexander muttered.

"Which part?" Theo gestured to everything around them.

Alexander was still mad at Theo, but he was more scared and worried than mad. He wanted to leave right now. But how could they? They couldn't even find Wil, and Aunt Saffronia was long gone. "Between the bat and the spa and the dreams of Lucy, this whole place is weird. Like, *bad* weird."

"Agreed." Theo folded her arms, glaring up at the new painting. "We're going to find out what, exactly, is going on at the Sanguine Spa. First things first," she said, taking charge, "we should—"

"There you are," a chipper voice drawled. Quincy flicked her lasso toward them. "The Count told me you were down here. You missed active meditation!"

"Aww, no. I'm so sad about that." Theo was not sad about it. Meditation—as Theo understood it—was sitting or lying perfectly still and quiet, while being very mindful about your thoughts instead of letting them swarm like a hive of bees. Meditation was used for a lot of other things, but that was what she had been working on with her mom before summer break.

It was basically the opposite of being active, though, so she didn't know what active meditation was, and she didn't care. She had mysteries to solve. And Alexander was still mad at her, so she had to distract him until he forgot.

"Well, at least I found you before the sauna. Hurry now, everyone else is waiting!" Quincy's lasso flicked impatiently, and Alexander found himself scurrying down the hallway for fear of literally being roped into participating.

Theo followed, eyeing the lasso jealously. "Why are the

activities mandatory?" Theo asked. "Why can't the kids join their parents?" She wanted to snoop in the adult spa.

"It's the only way to save—" Quincy paused, worry making her friendly face suddenly unfamiliar, then smiled bigger. "Well, the spa. Making it more spa-like. Making sure everyone is busy, busy, busy and happy, happy, happy."

"Was the spa not doing well before?" Alexander asked.

"It was dangerous."

"Dangerous?"

"I mean, in danger. Of shutting down. Here we are!" Quincy shot her lasso out and hooked a doorknob. She led them down a new hallway they'd never been in, to a sort of locker room. There were long wooden benches, as well as cubbies for their things. "Grab your salt scrubs. They're in that basket. We'll do those before the sauna." Quincy was distracted, trying to extricate the two sticky toddlers from where they'd both managed to climb into a single cubby. Eris walked up to her and whispered in Quincy's ear. Quincy listened, then shook her head. "No," she said. "Keep trying!"

"Trying what?" Ren shouted. "What are you whispering about?"

"We need to make a plan," Theo said, leaning close to Alexander as they walked over to the basket.

"No," Alexander said. "I don't want to."

"You're being a—" Theo started, but Alexander cut her off, holding up a bottle of salt.

Garlic salt.

"Why would they have us do a salt scrub with garlic salt?" he asked.

"Why would they have us do a salt scrub at all? What even is that?"

"No," Alexander said, scowling in frustration. "Theo. Think. We saw a vampire bat. There's a painting that keeps changing. We're not allowed out at night because it's not *safe*. The man in charge is the Count. We both had spooky dreams of the same little girl. And now we're supposed to cover ourselves in garlic, which everyone knows is to keep you safe from—"

"Vampires," Theo whispered. "Alexander, are we— Is this— Are we staying in a *vampire hotel?*"

CHAPTER
NINETEEN

Normally a sauna is a room that's super hot because someone decided sitting still and sweating is a good way to relax. They are, of course, wrong. Sweating while playing and having fun is good. Sitting still can be good, too, while watching a movie or picking a lock or reading. But sitting still doing nothing and sweating is a combination that should never, ever happen.

Fortunately for the children, saunas aren't safe for kids, so Quincy didn't actually heat it up. Which meant they were all sitting in a wooden box of a room for thirty minutes, at which point even Quincy couldn't pretend to be having fun.

"Let's play hide-and-go-seek," she declared, letting them all out of the heatless sauna. She grinned, twirling her rope. "And if I catch you, I *catch* you."

"Rules?" Alexander asked, because he was not about to break any more of them.

"You have to stay inside," Quincy said. "You can't go in any guest rooms. Once you pick a spot, you have to stay there, so no sneaking around and moving spots once I've cleared an area."

Theo knew exactly where she was going to go. This was the perfect opportunity to sneak into the grown-up spa area and spy.

"And what about the spa where the grown-ups are?" Alexander asked, raising an eyebrow at Theo because he knew what she was thinking and he was still mad at her.

"Absolutely off-limits!" Quincy said.

Theo stuck her tongue out at Alexander. He ignored her. She followed him as all the children scattered to find good hiding spots. Well, most of them scattered. Ren followed close behind them, creeping in what he thought was a stealthy way.

Theo stopped, turning to stare right at him. "Find your own spot," she said.

"You find your own spot!" he retorted.

"I am."

"So am I!"

"No, you're following us."

Ren glared. Then his face shifted, making him look sneaky. "Are you . . . looking for something?"

They weren't supposed to tell anyone about the scavenger hunt. That was what Quincy had told them.

"Yeah," Theo said. "A hiding spot. Duh."

Ren stomped one foot, then ran off. "I'll find it before you!"

"Ugh," Theo said, grabbing Alexander's arm to make him slow down. "Why did you make sure I couldn't go to the spa? Don't you want to know what's going on here?" she demanded.

"Of course I do! But I don't want to get in trouble doing it."

"You didn't mind getting in trouble at Fathoms of Fun! You broke out of their little jail room, and you tricked Edgaren't and the fake Mrs. Widow, and—"

"They were bad," Alexander said, scowling. "It's not breaking rules if the people who make the rules aren't supposed to be making them in the first place and can only make them because they've trapped the real person in charge in a tower. No one here is bad, Theo."

Theo scowled. "I don't like the Count."

"Yeah, but not liking someone doesn't make them bad. You don't like Ren, either, and he's not bad. He's just annoying."

"So annoying," Theo grumbled. "But what if the rules are keeping us from discovering something important? What if what happened to Mina's parents had something to do with the vampires? What if she's in danger, or we *all* are?"

Alexander didn't have an answer to that. "Let's just hide," he said. He was going to the kitchen, and Theo followed. While Theo was a notorious hider of food—any good cereal disappeared from the pantry, never to be seen again, and any leftover pizza was mysteriously impossible to find in the fridge until Theo would walk out of the kitchen, eating a perfectly cold and preserved piece—she wasn't necessarily a good hider of herself. Alexander, on the other hand, was very skilled at figuring out how to avoid being seen when he wanted to.

"We're going to hide in here," he said, climbing onto the counter and putting a hand on a cupboard.

"Are you sure climbing on the counters isn't against the rules?" Theo grumped.

Alexander turned to glare at her. Which was when they heard a high, haunting, laughing voice behind the cupboard door say *"Have you figured it out yet?"*

CHAPTER
TWENTY

Alexander scrambled back from the haunted cupboard but forgot he was on a counter. Lucky for him, Theo had fast reflexes, and even when they were fighting she wasn't about to let her brother fall. She caught him and set him on the floor, then jumped onto the counter and flung open the cupboard.

It was empty except for a jar of maraschino cherries, all the bright red liquid sucked out, leaving only a pile of sad cherries at the bottom.

"You heard her," Theo said.

"Yes," Alexander confirmed. He took a deep, shaking breath. "Thanks for catching me," he said softly.

Theo turned and sat on the counter, kicking her legs

161

against the bottom cupboards. She shrugged. "I always will."

"I know." He got onto the counter next to her, sitting at an angle to keep an eye on the still-open cupboard and make sure nothing—and no one—appeared in it. "I'm sorry I got so mad."

"I'm sorry I made you break a rule. I really didn't mean to. I just didn't think about it."

"I know."

"And I know it's important to you to follow rules whenever you can. I'll try to be more respectful of that."

"Thank you." Alexander knew it was hard for Theo to apologize, and not only had she apologized, she had said specifically what she did wrong, why it hurt Alexander, and what she was going to do to make sure it didn't happen again. He was proud of her.

"So what now?" Theo asked. "Because I need— I would like you to help me make a plan to figure things out."

"I'd like that, too," Alexander said. "But before anything else, we need to make sure Wil is okay. If this *is* a vampire hotel, then we have to keep her out of that spa."

Theo nodded. They set off toward Wil's room. They got to the bottom of the winding stairs when two pale hands shot out of the darkness and grabbed them, pulling them into a closet.

"What the—" Theo started, fists up, but then she saw it was Mina.

"Oh, hi, you two," Mina said, eyes big and almost glowing even in the darkness of the closet. "What were you doing in the kitchen?"

"We were hiding," Alexander said.

"From who?" she asked. "What's wrong?"

"Nothing's wrong. It's a game. A better game than the scavenger hunt, at least," Theo said. Alexander elbowed her sharply in the side. They weren't supposed to mention the scavenger hunt to Mina!

"A hunt?" Mina said, her voice rising. "What are you looking for? Is that why you were in the woods? Who told you to look for something? The Count?"

"What exactly is the Count the count of?" Alexander asked, trying to change the subject. "I didn't think we had counts in this country."

"It's a nickname. He was my parents' accountant."

"Ah, the Count!" Alexander laughed. "Because it's a short version of *accountant* and because he counts things!"

Mina nodded. "He worked for my parents for years. That's why they left everything to him."

Theo raised an eyebrow. "Must have been a really good accountant."

"I suppose so. Now, tell me: What is he having you look for?"

"We don't know," Alexander said, because it was the truth.

Mina sighed. "Listen. This is *important*. Don't look for anything, okay?"

"Why not?" Alexander asked.

"Because . . ." Mina searched the air for an answer—the thing adults do when they lie—and Theo's fists clenched. "Because you're here on a vacation! Just have fun. There's nothing to worry about and nothing to look for." Mina shooed them out of the closet. "I'm sorry I can't spend more time with you, but YOU KNOW I'M WATCHING YOU."

Alexander and Theo flinched. Before Alexander could promise they wouldn't go back to the door in the woods, Mina shook her finger at the ceiling above them.

"You're watching us?" Theo asked.

"Oh, uh. Watching out. Watching out for you! So you have a good time. Back to work now." She hurried down the hall.

"Why doesn't she want us to look?" Alexander asked.

"She was lying," Theo said, angry. "Whatever the Count and Quincy want us to look for, Mina doesn't want us to find."

"Are you sure she was lying?" Alexander's voice was soft and sad. Because he very rarely lied, he wasn't good at telling when someone else was lying, and he always assumed other people were honest.

"Yeah. I'm sure." Theo patted his hand. "Sorry."

"So who do we listen to? The Count, or Mina?"

"I like Mina, but . . . ," Theo trailed off.

"But she was lying to us."

"Right. And I don't like the Count, but . . ."

"But Quincy is working for him, and we like Quincy. And the Count does seem concerned for our safety. So who do we trust?" Alexander asked, at a loss.

"Ourselves," Theo stated, confident. "If we can't trust that anyone is telling us the truth, then we find out the truth for ourselves." She bumped Alexander with her shoulder, and he bumped her back. He wanted to take her hand—they often held hands without thinking when they were scared—but he suspected Theo was not scared right now.

"So we go and make sure Wil is safe, and then we figure out a way to get to that door in the woods," Alexander said. Because he was certain now that it was the thing they needed to find. "But we don't tell Quincy or the Count about it until after we know what's behind it," he added. Mina might have been lying to them, but he still didn't want to hurt her. And maybe it was nothing. Maybe it was a supply closet. In a rock. In the middle of the woods.

"Deal." They turned to go up the stairs when a rope shot out of nowhere, yanking them back and trapping them.

CHAPTER

TWENTY-ONE

Theo and Alexander didn't know which was worse: that they had been caught, or that they had been caught second and were now tied up with Ren. When Eris and the Js were found crouching beneath the lobby desk, Eris sighed. "We should have hidden in the big wooden box closet."

"The big wooden box closet?" Alexander asked, shifting to make room in the rope loop for the four new additions.

"Yeah," Joey said. "A closet filled with long wooden boxes with lids. We found it when we were looking for—"

Eris glared at him. "Shhh," she hissed.

"A closet full of long wooden boxes with lids," Alexander said, widening his eyes at Theo. "Almost like . . . coffins?"

Quincy laughed, listening in. "Well, if you want to be sinister, sure."

"We're always Sinister," Theo muttered, trying to get a J between herself and Ren. "Hey, Q. What do you know about vampires?" she asked as Quincy dragged them down another hallway.

"I know everything!" Ren said. "Go on. Ask me anything!"

"What do you know about vampires?" Theo repeated.

"They, uh, can turn into bats! And animals!"

"Not just animals," Quincy said. "Mist, too."

"Yeah, I knew that! Obviously! And they don't like the sun! Or onions!"

"Garlic," Alexander corrected him.

"That's what I meant!" Ren scowled. He was tripping them up, making everything take longer. It was hard enough walking lassoed together without someone like Ren refusing to coordinate his steps. "And they drink blood!"

Quincy nodded. "Sure do! But not always. Did you

know that in the Philippines, they have stories of Mandurugos, who look like normal girls by day, but at night they grow wings and their tongues turn long and hollow like needles? They don't drink blood, though."

"That's good." Alexander had never thought about just how full of blood he was, and how very much he wanted to stay full of blood.

"No," Quincy continued, "they eat hearts and livers and guts. And also snot from sick people. Cool, right?"

"Very . . . cool," Alexander said, his throat tight. He really wished they had never started this conversation and that he had never learned there were even more types of vampires. But now he knew, and he couldn't un-know, and he couldn't stop imagining tongues like needles. That was maybe even worse than fangs. He'd take a fang attack over that any day.

But he didn't want any type of attack. He tugged nervously on his collar, wishing he had worn a turtleneck. Or armor. Maybe he could pull some of the decorative armor off the wall.

Theo, however, was unconcerned with any of this new information. She thought the Mandurugos sounded pretty awesome. Wings *and* needle tongues? They made plain old vampires seem boring. She could totally knock a bat out of the air with a tennis racket, and mist wasn't scary at all.

Ren continued listing all the things they had already said about vampires as though he was the first one to say it. They stopped listening. Meanwhile, Quincy had tugged them up the winding stone steps they had dragged the trunk up just two days before. But the hallway was empty and the trunk was gone.

"Did Van H. arrive?" Theo asked, curious about the owner of the trunk.

"No, he's not here yet," Quincy said. She frowned at the door to the room where the trunk was sitting in the middle of the floor, locked tightly, holding the secrets of why this summer was such a sinister one instead of just a regular Sinister-Winterbottom one.

Quincy steered them back down the hallway past a side door. She opened it, and Theo and Alexander had one brief glorious glimpse of an incredible library before the cowgirl shut it again. "Didn't think the two sticky toddlers would be in there. And thank goodness, too. I can't imagine any books would survive them."

By the time Quincy had dragged them through all the parts of the building that weren't off-limits—the two sticky toddlers won hide-and-go-seek, but only by accident, having fallen asleep in the disappointing ballroom and blending in perfectly with the deflated balls scattered everywhere—it was time for Alexander to make dinner.

He used a *lot* of garlic, just to be safe.

While Quincy was distracted trying to feed the two sticky toddlers, Theo and Alexander shared a meaningful look. This was their chance! They stood and picked up their plates to take them in the kitchen and wash them. They might be suspicious of Mina now, but they were still going to do the right thing and clean up after themselves rather than leaving the mess for her.

The Count threw open the doors, nearly knocking them over on their way to the kitchen.

"Quincy!"

She jumped up. "Yes!"

"Get them their salt scrub and then off to bed!" he shouted.

"But it's only eight p.m.," Theo said, frowning. "And we need to wash our dishes."

"Nonsense!" The Count swept his arm out, knocking the dishes from their hands so they crashed to the floor. "That's Mina's job."

"Everything's Mina's job," Alexander said, scowling.

"Exactly! She must be kept completely occupied! Come now, off to bed."

"It's not even dark yet," Ren complained as Quincy undid the ropes around the two sticky toddlers with a single flick of her wrist.

"Precisely," the Count said, "which is why we must hurry and get you all locked in—I mean, settled in— before the sun sets."

Before anyone could protest, and without any parents to speak up on their behalf, the children were rushed down the hall, up the twisty stairs, and into the bunk room. "Get some rest," the Count said, standing in the doorway and surveying all the children with a worried scowl. His eyes landed on Theo and Alexander. "You'll need to work *much* harder tomorrow. Quincy, the door."

She grimaced. "I seem to have, uh, lost my key. I thought you unlocked it this morning."

He looked troubled. "No. Well, I still have my key, at least." With that, he slammed the door. And then there was an ominous metallic click as he locked them in.

Alexander tried not to feel scared that they were locked in a room in a spooky caspatle with possible vampires and definite bats roaming around and not an adult in sight to make sense of things or help them or just be comfortingly boring.

Theo turned around, buzzing with anger over the lock and annoyance that she still didn't know how to pick them. "Does anyone have any small metal tools?" she shouted. How could she have overlooked such a vital life skill as lockpicking? It was a tremendous personal failure, but also a failure of the school system to give her the education she really needed in order to succeed.

"Go to the window while it's still light enough to see," Alexander suggested softly. He knew Theo needed something to do or she'd explode. "Study the maze so we can get through it faster tomorrow."

Growling softly, Theo stalked over to the wide windows overlooking the back grounds of the caspatle and glared at the maze in concentration.

"Okay, everyone," Quincy said brightly. "Go do your salt scrubs; then I can lead you in a sleep meditation!"

Theo groaned. "Anything but that," she muttered.

Alexander went into one of the bathrooms. The faucets were shaped like mouths and the handles like claws. He picked up the bottle of garlic salt left on his sink. Feeling absolutely absurd, he sprinkled a little into his hair, then rubbed some vigorously on his neck. Then he brushed his teeth and changed into his pajamas. His mom had packed his favorite pair, worn and soft and cozy. Had she also packed a yo-yo? he wondered.

By the time he got out, Theo was already showered and waiting at their bunks. "I memorized it," she said.

Alexander sat on his bed, trying to brainstorm all the ways he could add garlic to their meals here. There was a clicking noise at the door, startling them all. It opened to reveal Mina holding a tray of milkshakes.

"Good-night milkshakes," she said brightly. "For a good night's sleep." Each milkshake had a single bright red cherry on top.

She set the tray on the table, then left, locking the door behind herself.

"Does it strike you as odd," Theo whispered to Alexander, "that a health spa would let us have milkshakes right before bedtime?"

"Almost like Mina is trying to win us over to her side. And she still has a key. Which means she could unlock or lock the door."

Alexander took his milkshake into the bathroom, eyeing it warily. As he brushed his teeth, he dumped the milkshake down the sink and ran the tap. The cherry dyed the water red as it swirled down the drain.

When Alexander went back into the big room, all the kids were in bed. And already asleep.

"No sleeping for us," Theo whispered.

"Yeah," Alexander agreed. Theo climbed onto his bed and they sat, side by side, staring out as darkness claimed the room around them, hiding whatever might be staring back.

CHAPTER
TWENTY-TWO

Theo startled awake, jerking upright from Alexander's shoulder. They were both still on his bed, but sitting alertly had turned to leaning sleepily had turned to sleeping soundly.

"Alexander," Theo whispered.

"I didn't start the fight with the monkey!" he said, blinking rapidly.

"I would never think you did." Theo patted his hand. "Wake up all the way."

Alexander's eyes cleared. "What's wrong?"

Theo pointed. She didn't know what had woken her up, but she knew why there was no way she could go back to sleep now. The door to the bunk room was, once again, wide open.

"Quincy?" Alexander asked.

"She lost her key, remember? And besides . . ." Theo pointed to where Quincy was fast asleep. She had abandoned her bed in favor of a hammock made of her lassos.

The floor was cold beneath Alexander's feet as he did a quick count. Every kid was there, and they were all asleep. "So who opened the door?" he whispered. "And why?"

Theo pulled on her shoes. Normally, they were a shoes-off-when-inside family, but there were different rules in caspatles. Especially caspatles that might be infested with vampires. "Let's go find out."

Alexander really, really didn't want to. But it was obvious whoever—or whatever—was out there could just as easily get in here. And, much to his relief, Theo reached out and took his hand. Which meant she was scared, too, even if she didn't show it.

Being scared with someone you trusted was always so much more pleasant than being scared alone.

"Let's check on Wil," he said.

They crept out the door and down the stairs. The rain clouds at last had disappeared, and the light of a full moon beamed in through the windows, stark and white. That, combined with a few flickering candles mounted on the walls, meant they had just enough light as they crept down a familiar hallway to get to the lobby. And just enough light to see that Alexander's least favorite painting had, once again, changed.

This time, it was a painting of the Sanguine Spa building. But it had been painted from a weird angle, with the building in the distance at the very top. The cliffs Wil had almost wandered off were the focus of the painting.

"Do you feel that?" Theo asked. She was always hyper-aware of her own body. Where it was, how it felt, what was touching it. Right now, a breeze was touching it. She looked around for air vents but didn't see any. "It feels like it's coming from the painting."

Alexander didn't want to get closer. But Theo was right. There was definitely a current of frigid air coming from the painting. Alexander took a deep breath and reached up to wiggle the frame. It didn't budge. Usually paintings were unstable, hung by a single nail. Which meant they were nearly always slightly, maddeningly crooked. Alexander nudged. Then he tugged. The frame didn't move so much as a centimeter.

A hunch seized him. "Help me drag that bench over here!" Once they got it in place, Alexander stood on it. He felt all around the edges of the frame and—there! "Hinges! This isn't only a painting," he said. "It's a door! But I can't find a latch to open it."

"But why is it a door?" Theo asked. "And where does it lead?"

"I knew it wasn't a regular painting," Alexander said as his fingers found something resting on top of the frame. He picked up the object, and his heart squeezed with fear. "Harker Suite," he whispered.

"Yeah, that's Wil's room; we'll get going," Theo agreed.

Alexander held up the key to Wil's room, neatly labeled *Harker Suite*. "Harker Suite," he repeated.

"What's that doing here?"

"I don't know, but let's hurry." Alexander hopped off the bench, and they shoved it back into place, then ran as quietly as they could through the lobby and into the hallway that led to the stairs that led to the Harker Suite.

"Why are there are so many sets of stairs in this stupid spa?" Theo huffed. She loved running and exercise, but this was an awful lot of stairs between her and making sure her sister was safe. And any amount of stairs in the middle of the night is too many, as kids who sleep on a different floor of the house than the bathroom can tell you.

Theo tried the doorknob when they got to Wil's room. "Unlocked," she whispered. They hurried inside and rushed past the open bathroom door to Wil's bed.

Wil's very empty bed.

"Where is she?" Alexander said. Wil's bag was open on the floor, the contents scattered.

Theo ran her hands through her hair, making it stick up even more wildly. "Maybe there's a spa activity? In the middle of the night?"

Alexander was scared, but he was more scared for Wil than he was for himself. At least he had Theo. Wil didn't have anyone to look out for her, and they hadn't been able to warn her. She had no idea what threats lurked in this place.

"Where should we look for her?" Theo asked.

"The last two times we saw her were in the spa and the lobby. So we start there."

Theo nodded. "The lobby does have a computer. She loves computers. Almost as much as she loves Rodrigo. *Wait.* Rodrigo!" Theo ran back into the room and did a quick search, which made her feel much better.

"She's probably okay," Theo said, taking Alexander's hand in the hallway. "She didn't leave Rodrigo behind."

"Oh, thank goodness." Alexander shared Theo's relief. "And that means I know how to find her! There's a phone in the kitchen. We can call her."

"Genius." They hurried down the stairs, through a hallway, through the lobby, and to the kitchen. They didn't dare turn on any lights, but a shaft of moonlight from a window fell right on the phone.

Most people these days don't have any phone numbers memorized, but Alexander was not most people. He had Wil's phone number memorized, his mom's, his dad's, Aunt Saffronia's, poison control, a toll-free number to check the weather, and even the local pizza delivery place. He had good priorities.

Wil picked up immediately. "This is Wil-o'-the-Wisp," she said, but her voice sounded hard and angry in a way Alexander had never heard, "and you had better have my information or I will *destroy* you."

"Wil?" Alexander whispered, very confused.

"Alexander?" Wil's voice changed. "What are you doing? Where are you?"

"We went to your room but you weren't there, so we were worried. The hotel is—"

"Get back to bed!" Wil snapped. "It isn't safe to be wandering around at night!"

Alexander wanted to ask Wil what, exactly, *she* was doing out, then. But before he could ask, she hung up. Alexander frowned down at the phone before hanging it up, too. "She's safe. I guess."

"Well, as long as she's safe." Theo's smile was as wide and bright as a gravel path in the moonlight. "This seems like a perfect time to get to that door in the woods without anyone noticing."

"What?" Alexander shook his head. "No. It's dark!"

"That's perfect! No one will see us!"

"But how will *we* see?"

"The moonlight!"

"And what about the slugs?"

"What *about* the slugs?" Theo asked, puzzled, continuing to live in oblivious peace, never wondering about the relative threat level of slugs. She took Alexander's hand and pulled him out into the hallway. "Come on, it'll be—"

Mina's voice drifted to them, the echo of the lobby making it sound like she was all around them. "I know you're there," she sang out, her tone both haunting and teasing at the same time. "I know you're there, and I'm going to find you. . . ."

"Okay, change of plans," Theo whispered. "Let's go hide in our beds until morning."

The Sinister-Winterbottom twins were in perfect agreement.

CHAPTER
TWENTY-THREE

The Count appeared in their doorway at dawn. "Why wasn't this locked? Is everyone accounted for? Everyone safe?"

Alexander thought that was a much more ominous greeting than "Good morning!" or "How did everyone sleep?"

"Yes, sir!" Quincy chirped. Theo and Alexander disagreed with her assessment of *safe*. They had spent the rest of the long, sleepless night keeping guard.

"Good. Get them busy," the Count commanded. "And you two," he said, fixing a sharp eye on Theo and Alexander. "I expect you to do much better today." With that, he left.

"What did he mean?" Ren asked. "Are you doing a bad job at something? I knew it! I knew I was better than you!"

"Gotta go make breakfast." Alexander grabbed Theo's arm and tugged her out of the room. As soon as they were free, he started running. "Wil," he said.

"Wil," Theo agreed. Their sister might have answered her phone last night, but she didn't let them tell her how much danger she was in. After all, they'd already found a vampire bat hanging around outside her room. She needed to know to protect herself.

They raced to her room and knocked, but there was no answer. "Still unlocked," Theo whispered, which made sense, since she had the key in her own pocket.

The twins crept in, unnerved by how quiet and dark it was inside. The curtains were drawn, so it took them getting very close to the bed to see that—thankfully—Wil was in it this time. She was wrapped up in her blankets, like she had been tossing and turning. Rodrigo was plugged in to charge but remained clutched in her hand, resting on the pillow next to her. A text popped up, lighting the screen and illuminating Wil's face. She had dark circles under her eyes, and, on her neck, two perfectly circular red bumps.

"Oh no," Alexander and Theo whispered at the same time.

They were too late.

"Wil!" shouted Theo, shaking Wil's shoulder. "Wake up!"

Wil groaned, flinging her free hand through the air to swat Theo away.

"Wil!" Alexander joined Theo. He needed Wil to wake up, to be okay.

"Get out, twerps," Wil growled, peeking one blood-shot eye open at them before rolling over.

Alexander couldn't think. What should they do with a teen vampire sister? What would his parents do if they were here? He wished desperately that they were, and then immediately stopped that wish. He was glad his parents weren't here, weren't in that spooky spa, weren't whatever Wil was now. The rush of gratitude that at least his parents were safe was enough to calm him down.

Theo grabbed Alexander's hand and dragged him out of the room and into the hallway. Just as she suspected, this door locked from the outside *or* the inside, the same way the bunk room did. Which meant that they could use the key to lock Wil in. So Theo did just that.

"Now she can't go to the spa. And she can't get hurt, or

hurt . . ." Theo trailed off, not willing to say she was worried maybe Wil would hurt someone else. Wil *wasn't* a vampire. She couldn't be. The bees were in a frenzy, their hive smashed to pieces, too many feelings to understand or contain any of them.

There existed some problems that were too big for twelve-year-olds. Even wildly brave and prudently cautious, extremely clever twelve-year-olds. "I think we should call Aunt Saffronia," Alexander said. She wasn't a responsible adult by any measure, but she was the closest thing they had right now.

They hurried to the kitchen but froze outside the door. They could hear Mina inside, humming to herself.

"Lobby has a phone," Theo whispered. They backed slowly away. Fortunately, the lobby was as empty as Aunt Saffronia's fridge had been when they first arrived in her kitchen.

Alexander picked up the phone behind the desk and dialed Aunt Saffronia's number. Like when he called her from Fathoms of Fun, it rang for an eternity. Finally, the dull ring was replaced by crackling static.

"Hello?" Alexander's voice was timid, like he was calling into a dark cave and afraid of what might answer back.

"Alexander," Aunt Saffronia said.

"Yes! Yes, it's me. Listen, something is wrong here. I think you should come pick us up."

"Have you found what we needed?"

"What? Are you talking about the scavenger hunt? It doesn't make any sense! There aren't enough clues. And Wil's in trouble."

Aunt Saffronia answered as though she hadn't heard him. "We need to look closer. You *must* be able to look closer. I cannot come and retrieve you until you can. I wish there was another way. Your mother thought there might be, and look where that got her."

"What? Where? Where did it get her?" Alexander demanded. They still didn't know where their parents were, or why they hadn't called, or why Wil couldn't get ahold of them.

"Exactly. Where *did* it get her? Where, oh, where, foolish, sweet Syringa?" Aunt Saffronia went silent.

Alexander was afraid she hung up, but he wasn't ready to hang up yet. "So we're on our own?" he asked.

"You are never on your own. You are Sinisters, and Sinisters have each other. We are all depending on you. *Find what was lost.*" Her voice took on that same low rumble of thunder quality it had sometimes. Alexander felt the command more than heard it. But then the static cut off. The call was over.

"What did she say?" Theo asked.

Alexander slowly hung up the phone. "She said we can't go until we find what we need. That we have to look closer. Find what was lost."

"She wants us to win the scavenger hunt?" Theo asked, aghast.

"Well, she wants us to find *something*, at least. But I think we know exactly what we need to find." Alexander paused, putting a hand on his throat as he swallowed hard against the lump of fear there. "We need to find proof of vampires."

"And figure out who the vampire is. Because we've seen Mina outside in the daylight."

"But it was cloudy," Alexander said, wishing he could agree that it definitely wasn't Mina. "Plus, there could be more than one vampire. I mean, the man who runs this place calls himself the Count, which seems definitely vampirish." Alexander hated the idea of vampires, plural, even more than vampire, singular.

"Okay. We figure out the vampires, and that leads us to figuring out how to save Wil."

Alexander tried to replace all his fear with determination. Because Aunt Saffronia was right. They weren't alone. They had each other, and vampires or not, no one messed with one Sinister-Winterbottom without messing with all of them.

CHAPTER
TWENTY-FOUR

Alexander was sitting calmly on the chair in front of the lobby desk because sitting helped him focus. Theo was pacing like a tiger because moving helped her focus.

One thing both twins had in common was that when they were too worried or too filled with emotions, having a plan gave their brains something to do besides panic. Wil might be turning into a vampire, and Aunt Saffronia wouldn't come get them until they found a way to look closer. Fine. They were good at finding things, and they were going to find out what exactly was going on at the Sanguine Spa.

Theo cracked her knuckles with a terrible popping

sound she knew Alexander hated, but Alexander also knew Theo did it when she was nervous, so he forgave it this time. "We have to figure out how to avoid Mina long enough to get through that door."

Alexander nodded, glum. Wil was the oldest sibling and should be watching out for them, but for the second time in as many weeks, they were scrambling to solve a mystery in order to keep her safe. Alexander wondered if they should have shown their mother's letter to Wil. But how would that help? Sure, Alexander had ended up needing the reminder to be cautious, and Theo had needed the boost of confidence in her own bravery, but why did Wil need to be told to use her phone? She never *didn't* use her phone.

"Wait," Alexander said. "We know Mina's in the kitchen right now, right?"

"Let's check." They tiptoed to the kitchen door. Sure enough, Mina was inside, singing and laughing, carrying on one side of a conversation.

"You can't see the maze from the kitchen window." Alexander was happy that his time in the kitchen had been put to good use in addition to making delicious food for everyone.

"Let's go!" Theo said. The twins slipped outside, the

humidity embracing them with greedy joy. The air was positively green, humming with life, but also silent. They were alone out here. They raced around the side of the building, past all the activities meant to keep them so busy they couldn't notice anything suspicious going on, and then they arrived at the entrance to the maze. Just before they stepped inside, Theo turned and looked back at the caspatle.

There was a face pressed against a window, staring down at them. The glass was too thick for Theo to see who it was. But *someone* knew they were out here.

She pulled out her timer, her heart picking up speed. "It takes Mina seven minutes, so if that was her, it'll take her a few minutes to get down here and then seven minutes to get through. Which means we have to make it through as fast as possible!" She started the timer, made sure Alexander was still at her side, and ran.

Theo's brain, while frequently not great at following directions or remembering important things like putting on socks before shoes or asking permission, was very, very good at directions and mazes. And her body was very, very good at running.

Alexander kept up as best he could, all their turns a blur. He'd never make it through alone, but he didn't need to because he had Theo. They burst through the maze on the other side, gasping for air.

"Five minutes!" Theo crowed, holding up the timer. Then she reset it. "We have a head start, but it won't last long. We need to get through that door fast. Come on."

They slipped down the trail, avoiding the slugs that seemed to be spelling out a warning in a language all their own. Alexander imagined it was Morse code for slugs. Dash-dash-dash-dash-dash, every *dash* standing for "turn around and follow the rules."

Soon enough they were at the boulders. Theo tried the door. It was, unsurprisingly, locked. She looked at the timer. Two minutes had already passed. Her bees were getting unruly again. "What do we do?" she asked. "Punch in random numbers and hope we find the right code?"

Alexander looked closer at the keypad. Just like an old phone, it had letters beneath each number. "What if the code *isn't* a set of numbers? What if it's a word?"

"But what word could it be? We don't have any clues."

"Well, it'll probably be four letters. So that narrows it down." But not by much. There were many, many four-letter words in the world. Alexander thought about the spa's former owners. What would *his* parents use as a passcode? Their kids' names! Though he really hoped his parents would never use his own name as a passcode because that would mean shortening it to four letters, which was Alex, which he refused to answer to.

But the Bloods had two daughters with four-letter names. Alexander held his breath, and typed the numbers corresponding to *LUCY*: 5-8-2-9.

Nothing happened.

He tried *MINA*: 6-4-6-2. Nothing happened. His shoulders fell. His brilliant idea hadn't been so brilliant after all. He had failed. "We don't have any other clues," he said. "I can't just guess it."

"Wait," Theo said. "*A guessing game.* Like the one from my dream. What's her sixth-favorite animal?" What if it wasn't just a bizarre question? What if it was a clue? What if it was . . .

Theo punched in 2-2-8-7. The code to spell out *BATS*.

There was a click, and the door swung inward.

CHAPTER
TWENTY-FIVE

lexander hadn't thought past getting the door open because he never really thought they *would* get the door open.

But now, gazing into a stair-lined tunnel going down like the throat of some dread beast, waiting to swallow them whole, Alexander realized that had been a huge failure of imagination. He was now making up for it at record speed, his mind cycling through infinite possibilities of what could be at the bottom, each more terrible than the last. Slugs. Vampires. Vampire slugs. An endless pit they'd fall down forever while vampire slugs laughed at them for every embarrassing mistake they'd ever made.

"Could be storage," Theo said, her tone chipper. She'd

always assumed they'd be able to get in. *And* she had guessed that weird voice's sixth-favorite animal, after beating Mina's time through the maze! She had no idea what would be at the bottom of those stairs but couldn't wait to find out. She was on a total winning streak and wished she could rub it in Ren's face.

"Do we be brave, or do we be cautious?" Alexander whispered. That was the problem of always being together. If he was *supposed* to be cautious, and Theo was *supposed* to be brave, but they were making the same decision, how did they know which to settle on? Mina had wanted to keep them out of here. Sure, she might be a vampire, but he still liked her. She was sad, but her sadness hadn't turned her sour or mean, and that said a lot about a person. So did they listen to her? Or did they go against what she told them? Did he trust her, or not?

Theo, in contrast to Alexander, had a single thought in her head:

Down!

So, as usual, Theo made the decision for them. She stepped through the door and was halfway down the stairs before Alexander had even crossed the threshold.

The temperature inside was an immediate relief, several degrees cooler than the air outside. "Maybe it's part of the spa," Alexander whispered. "That one room sort of looked like a cave anyway. Maybe we'll see all the parents with, like, seaweed fingernails and slug-slime facials." Admittedly, he had no idea what happened in spas. Neither seaweed fingernails nor slug-slime facials were real things. Yet. All they needed was a celebrity spokesperson, though, and that would change.

Still, even imagining the spa wasn't calming his nerves. Alexander pictured the adults lifting seaweed-clad hands like zombies, walking toward him, moaning, forcing him to join them in the spa. He didn't want a slug-slime facial. He didn't want any sort of facial! "Don't let them make me get a facial, Theo," he whispered, grabbing hold of the back of her shirt.

"No one touches your face unless you want them to," Theo whispered, her voice fierce. Sometimes, when Alexander was scared, it made her even braver. She was ready and willing to defeat anyone at the bottom of these stairs who might touch Alexander's face. Though she didn't *quite* understand why that was what he was afraid of. She thought it was much more likely that they would find a sheer drop off a cliff, or else vampires. One or the other.

At last, they got to the bottom of the stairs. There was a rugged rock face ahead of them, black and wet, and a carved archway to their left. But when they went through it, all they found was a cave. A giant, soaring cave, without a wave pool to be seen. Which was probably for the best because it would have been even more confusing to find a wave pool under here. Though at least the twins knew what to do with wave pools in creepy caves.

While the stairs had obviously been carved on purpose, with a strip of lights and a metal railing added for safety—details that actually *did* make Alexander feel a little better, because surely vampires wouldn't be concerned with stair safety, would they?—the cave seemed entirely natural. The floor was rough and uneven, with lots of shiny spots. There was an ammonia-like smell, which meant it smelled like cleaning products, but cleaning products if the cleaning products themselves were moldy and dirty and gross.

It was, in short, unpleasant.

At the far end of the cave, they could see a hint of light coming from around a bend. Maybe there was an exit other than these stairs.

And that made Alexander realize something horrible:

there wasn't any daylight coming from behind them. He hurried back up the stairs, but they had made a huge mistake. They hadn't propped open the door. It was shut, and locked, and he couldn't get it open.

"Well?" Theo whispered.

Alexander slowly went down to where Theo was waiting. "We better find another way out."

"On it," Theo said, full of confidence. She had found a way in after all. Finding a way out should be even easier. But as she took a step onto the cave floor, there was a rustling noise. She stopped. Alexander stopped. They both stood perfectly still. *There*, again, a slight rustle, but it was impossible to tell where the noise came from. It echoed around the cave like it was tiptoeing to their ears.

"What do you think that is?" Alexander wished there was more light. "Actually, no. I don't want to know."

"Remember that painting?" Theo asked.

Alexander remembered all the paintings. The one with Mrs. Blood and her fuzzy bat friend that came to life. The one with Mr. Blood and the way he watched them, menacing. The one with the whole family . . . in a cave . . . with the roof of the cave looking fuzzy.

And bat-like.

"We need to get out of here," Alexander whispered, squeezing Theo's hand.

"Come on. Toward the light." They carefully crossed the smelly cave floor. Around the bend in the cave passageway, they were nearly blinded by the brilliance of full daylight. But that was the problem. There was daylight right in front of them . . . and nothing else. Just a sheer drop into the sky.

"This is the cliff!" Theo said.

"Yes. Obviously," Alexander agreed, tugging her backward.

"We need to get out of here."

"Yes. Definitely."

"And the only door we know of is locked."

"Yes. Unfortunately."

"And we have a sheer drop to a rock-covered forest floor this way."

"Yes. Terrifyingly."

"But . . ." Theo leaned out—too far for Alexander's comfort—and looked up. She reached into her pocket and withdrew Quincy's rope, already tied with a loop around the end. "We're not that far from the cliff top."

"No. Definitely not," Alexander said.

"We don't have any other options. I really think this has a chance of working."

"No!" Alexander shook his head. "We can go back up the stairs, try to open the door again. Or just wait. Maybe someone will come along and open it."

"I don't think we can wait for that. Or that we *should* wait for that. Whoever opens the door will be someone who doesn't want us in here. Alexander, I can do this." Theo wasn't being reckless. She was being reckful. She knew exactly what she was capable of, how good she was at climbing. And she knew, right down to her already-wriggling toes, that she could do this.

The rustling in the cave behind them intensified.

"Let me anchor you while you throw it," Alexander said, making up his mind. If Theo was going to be brave, he'd be as cautious as he could on her behalf. He grabbed her left hand, holding tight as she leaned out into the open air. She twirled the lasso a few times, then threw it, sending it sailing upward. It fell back down. She tried again. It fell back down.

"One more try," she whispered. Alexander didn't know whether to hope it worked or hope it didn't.

"Wait!" Alexander said. "Attach it here!" He pointed

to where a stalagmite was jutting out over the opening. "That way, you can climb down, instead of up. And I can make sure the rope stays tightly fastened."

"It'll take me longer to find a way up and around to the door to let you out." Neither of them suggested Alexander try to climb down after her, because they both knew he couldn't.

The idea of being all alone in this dark cave scared Alexander, but not as much as the danger Theo would be facing if she climbed up instead of down. Cautious and brave, together. "I'll be okay. Just go as fast as you can. *After* you reach the ground! Go very, very slowly to get to the ground!"

Theo grinned and nodded, squeezing Alexander in a hug. They attached the lasso to the stalagmite. The end of the rope reached almost all the way down. "I got this," Theo said, both to Alexander and herself. She turned around, grabbed the rope, and rappelled.

It wasn't quite the rappelling she had imagined, with ropes and pulleys and helmets and all the things that would make it safe to go fast. But it was definitely a challenge that required her complete and absolute attention, which was her favorite type of challenge.

Alexander watched, his stomach tied in even tighter knots than the rope. Theo went slowly, carefully, hand by hand down the rope, with her feet braced against the rock to control her descent. And then she reached the end.

Alexander held his breath.

Theo dropped.

CHAPTER
TWENTY-SIX

Theo barely had time to wonder where the ground was before she landed.

"I'm okay!" she shouted, then immediately cringed. No loud noises by the vampire bat cave. She did double thumbs-up, instead.

Alexander waved and pulled the rope up, carefully looping it around his shoulder. He didn't have anything to do while he waited for Theo. Except explore, and he really, really didn't want to explore. He stayed by the opening as long as he could stand it, appreciating the fresh air and the light. But after a few minutes, he began to worry that Theo would get to the door faster than he expected and he wouldn't be waiting for her. So he turned and tiptoed back into the cave. He looked all around the walls, in part to avoid looking at the ceiling, which he suspected was riddled with bats, and to avoid looking at the floor, which he knew was riddled with bat poop.

"Guano," he whispered to himself, because bat poop was so fancy it even had its own name. Doubtless his dad would have come up with an excellent pun.

I guano know why you're in a cave filled with vampire bats.

Alexander wondered the same thing.

Are you guano take all day down there?

Alexander really hoped not.

Was anyone guano tell you about the door in the wall?

Alexander stopped short. Now that his eyes were adjusted to the darkness again, he saw what they had missed their first trip through the cave. There was, in fact, a door in the wall. It was all the way across the cave, on the opposite side of the stairs. They had been too focused on the light at the end of the tunnel. Unbeknownst to them, Aunt Saffronia would have found that hilarious, as Sinisters were known for ignoring lights at the ends of tunnels.

The new door left Alexander with a conundrum, a fancy word for a puzzling problem. His mother always called things *conundrums* instead of problems because, as she put it, a *conundrum* sounded like much more fun.

Should he try the door in the cave wall or wait at the stairs for Theo? If he could get out faster through the door, he could help Theo. But then again, if he went the wrong way, they might miss each other out in the forest, and she would end up back at the cave and not know where he went, and he would end up lost, devoured by vampire slugs.

But Alexander's choice was once again made for him.

The mystery door swung open. Alexander couldn't even hide because the beam of light from the door landed on him like a spotlight. And when he saw who came out, he didn't know whether to be relieved or worried.

He lifted one hand to wave cautiously at Mina.

But instead of Mina's smile, he was greeted with a look of absolute anger and horror. "WHAT ARE YOU DOING HERE?" Mina shouted, and it was *very* clear that this time she was yelling at Alexander and Alexander alone. She slapped a hand over her mouth, her eyes going even wider as she looked straight up.

Alexander followed her stare to see the roof of the cave—the *entire* roof of the cave—beginning to writhe and wriggle and come alive.

207

"Alexander!" Theo shouted from the top of the stairs. Alexander turned and sprinted for the stairwell.

"Stop!" Mina shouted.

"Don't stop!" Theo yelled.

It wasn't a hard decision to make. Much as Alexander always tried to listen to people in charge, he wasn't about to stop. Because now it wasn't just the cave ceiling that was alive with movement. The air was filling with little bodies, flapping and flinging themselves with chaotic abandon.

Alexander put his hands over his neck as he ran up and up. There were a few bats above him, darting and wheeling through the small space, but he made it to the top without being bitten. Theo was waiting, holding the door open.

It had taken everything she had not to race down the stairs to help Alexander. But she knew the door would close, and then they'd be in the same situation all over again. Alexander would have been proud of her using caution, but at the moment, he was too busy being afraid of being bitten by a vampire bat.

He flew through the door—but not literally, like a bat would, only figuratively, like a terrified twelve-year-old

trying not to be bitten by a vampire in bat form would—
and Theo slammed it shut behind him.

"This is—" Alexander started, trying to catch his
breath.

"Bad," Theo continued.

"Super bad."

"The absolute baddest."

"The absolute battest," Alexander finished, because
even in his terrified state, he couldn't help but go for the
easy pun.

"Come on." Theo sprinted toward the caspatle. Even
though she had climbed down a cliff, then run along it
until she found a path up, and then run along that path
back to the cave entrance door, she felt like she could do it
all a million more times if she had to. Whatever it took to
keep Alexander safe. "We have to find somewhere to hide
from Mina and the Count while we decide what to do."

"Right." Alexander was in complete agreement. It
helped that Theo's plan was hiding, instead of something
like taking on an army of vampires.

Really, Theo would have been willing to do that,
but she wanted to be prepared. Right now she couldn't
think. All her bees were buzzing, filling her up. She

was afraid her chest might turn into a cave of bats if she didn't figure out a way to settle herself down. At least bees buzzed with a purpose—to find food, to sting threats, to build things. If she had *bats* in her chest flinging themselves around in absolute chaos, how would she ever manage?

"I don't want to be turned into a vampire!" she said as they entered the maze and she clicked her timer to make sure they were going fast enough to beat Mina.

"Me neither." Alexander and Theo didn't usually agree 100 percent on anything, except that raisins had no place in cookies and churros should be far more common, but they absolutely agreed on this. They raced through the maze. Theo barely had time to feel triumphant that their time was now under five minutes before they were running past the lobby. Then, not knowing where else to go, they ran down the portrait hall.

"Do you see that?" Alexander gasped. "It's a painting *of a bat!*"

"Keep going!" Theo cautioned. "Where do we hide?"

"Library!" Alexander said. He always felt safe in libraries, and the one at Fathoms of Fun had helped them. They found the stairs they had dragged the trunk up, then followed them to the top. They pushed open the first hallway door to see a stack of long, narrow wooden boxes.

"Not this one!" Alexander said, his voice strangled with stress. He did *not* want to hide in the coffin closet.

Theo threw open the next door and instantly felt better. "We'll be safe in here," she said, closing the door behind them and leaning against it.

Alexander turned and took in the room with a sigh of relief. Nothing bad ever happened in libraries.

Unfortunately, there's a first time for everything.

CHAPTER
TWENTY-SEVEN

The library was precisely what a library should be, which is filled with books. Anything else in a library is a bonus. Fortunately, this library also had lots of bonuses. The shelves went from the floor all the way up to the high ceiling, which, like every other ceiling in the hotel, was crisscrossed with exposed wooden beams. There were several leather reading chairs and several full-length windows suffusing the space with warm light. The wood floors were muffled with a deep red carpet, and—and this was the part that had Theo's head about to explode with joy, all thoughts of vampires and bats and vampire bats flung out of her much in the way that nighttime flings bats out of their caves—*ladders*.

The bookshelves had *ladders*.

Not just any ladders, either. Not step stools, or dinky metal ladders, or even ladders like the ones on the bunk beds, bolted into place and immovable. No. These shelves had *ladders on wheels*. There were wheels at the bottoms, and the tops hooked over the shelves, with tiny wheels that ran along a track. Which meant that someone—Theo, in this case—could take a running leap, catch a ladder, and fly along the shelves all the way to the wall.

"It's so beautiful," she whispered, feeling much the same way that Alexander felt when he looked at Mina, an overwhelming mix of emotions that made it difficult to function. She felt like laughing, and crying, but most of all she felt like riding a ladder down an entire wall of books and shelves.

So she did.

Alexander couldn't even chide her to be careful. He did have several thoughts—she could bonk her head, or the ladder could come undone and she could fall, or an errant book could be sticking out too far and smack Theo as she passed it—but even Alexander's worst-case scenarios weren't really all that *worst* when it came to the sheer joy of watching Theo live out a dream she didn't know she had.

"Do you want a turn?" she gasped, breathless with happiness and wanting to share it with her brother.

"I'll take one later." As amazing as library ladders were, they were in serious trouble. He needed to focus. Alexander paced, his hands behind his back. "This is the hotel's library. Which means it was stocked by Mina's family. And, since we now know Mina knows about the vampire bats, and therefore the potential vampires, we have to assume she has more information. And that she won't willingly tell us." Alexander sighed. It made him sad to think of Mina this way. Had he really been this wrong about her?

Theo nodded. "I'll bet we can find something here." She still rode the ladder back and forth, but this time with less reckless and more reckful abandon. She was getting good at being reckful. She scanned titles, letting her eyes skim as the ladder carried her past shelf after shelf. Then she went down a rung and did it on the next level of shelves. There were lots of titles—so, so many. It really was an excellent library, and under non-vampiric circumstances she would take her time.

Well, no, that wasn't true. Under non-vampiric circumstances, she'd spend the whole day riding the ladder.

At least this way, she still got to ride the ladder while also searching the fiction titles for a book that might help.

Alexander looked on the opposite wall. It also had a ladder, but Alexander opted to browse the old-fashioned way, with his feet on the ground. He didn't trust himself to be able to read while also worrying about falling or breaking something.

Unlike Theo's shelves, this group seemed less geared toward guests. There were far fewer mysteries, thrillers, romances, and graphic novels. The books here were old. A lot of them were textbooks from decades ago, like someone couldn't bear to throw away a book, even if it was *Hematology 101*. That hardly seemed like a page-turner. Alexander wasn't sure what hematology was, other than the -ology of hemat-. There was also a copy of *A History of Summer Camps and the Unexplained Disappearances of Various Campers in the Mountainous Lake Regions*. It wasn't a book he'd ever choose to read—it sounded scary. He vowed never to go to summer camp in the mountainous lake regions.

He trailed his fingers down the spines, wondering if anything was actually going to be helpful, when he stopped.

"Theo," he said.

She finished her latest pass and turned toward him, swinging the ladder back. "Yeah?"

Alexander pulled the book free. It was well worn, the letters of the title so cracked that half of them were illegible. But what he could see confirmed his worst, most unbelievable fears.

The Care and Keeping of Vampir— the spine read before the letters were rubbed off. But Alexander could fill in the blanks without any problem at all.

Vampires. The care and keeping of *vampires*.

"We were right!" Theo crowed. Then she stopped. "We were . . . right?" Even when she had been afraid of vampires, she hadn't *really* believed in them. It was one thing to be afraid of ghosts, or a monster under your bed, or an alligator that would come up and bite your bottom if you flushed while you were still sitting on the toilet. It was another thing to really, truly believe those things existed. Sure, you might hold your breath passing cemeteries, or turn off your light and jump into bed as quickly as possible, or always, always make sure you were safely clear of the toilet before flushing it, but those were *just in case*. Not because you actually thought those things were real.

Alexander held the book away from his body, as though, much like a toilet alligator, it might bite him. "It was with all these textbooks."

"The nonfiction section," Theo said. She and Alexander shared a heavy look. Unless it was an egregious mis-shelving incident in an otherwise very well-organized library, whoever put *The Care and Keeping of Vampires* in nonfiction considered it to be factual.

"I think you and I should OH NO NOT NOW!" Alexander shouted, staring up at the ceiling with wide eyes, where Lucy—Mina's sister from the painting, the little girl who had appeared to both Theo and Alexander in what they now realized were not, in fact, dreams, and the little girl who was definitely, for sure, absolutely not at the spa and possibly not even alive—waved calmly at them.

CHAPTER
TWENTY-EIGHT

Theo and Alexander ran. Fast. Out of the library, down the hall, down the stairs, down the hall, through the lobby, down the hall, and finally into the disappointing ballroom, where they hid behind several large partially inflated exercise balls.

"Lucy isn't gone," Theo said.

"And she can climb straight up walls. And hang out in ceilings."

"All those times Mina yelled!"

"Except for the times she was actually yelling at us, she was yelling at Lucy! And this morning, talking to herself in the kitchen. I'll bet she *wasn't* talking to herself."

"Maybe last night she was with Lucy?" Theo said.

"Either way, Lucy is here, when the person in charge—the Count—doesn't know about it. So Mina's been hiding her. Why would Mina do that if there wasn't a good, by which I mean bad, reason? Like, a vampiric reason?" Alexander had shoved the vampire book into his jacket pocket, and it was digging into his side as he crouched. He wanted to read about the vampires, but Mina and Lucy might find them at any moment.

"I mean, their last name is Blood. We should have known! The Count told us it was dangerous to be out at night, and locked us in, even if it didn't work. And Quincy warned us not to go in the maze. Maybe that's why they wanted everyone to be in groups, too! Safety in numbers."

"I spent a lot of time alone in the kitchen." Alexander shuddered, thinking of all the times he could have been bitten. "And I'm pretty sure Lucy was in the cupboard sometimes. Drinking the bright red maraschino cherry juice. She must have been, I don't know, misting in and out or whatever. However she was doing it doesn't matter. We have to get Wil and get out of here."

"No, we have to defeat the vampires and save everyone and find what Aunt Saffronia needs," Theo disagreed.

One plan based in caution, the other in bravery. Both were reasonable. Well, no. Only the running away one was reasonable. If one ever finds oneself in a hotel surrounded by vampires, running away is wise.

Alexander shook his head. Once again, his mother's advice was less than helpful. If he was cautious and Theo was brave, they'd make different choices. And they certainly couldn't split up. "Whichever choice we make, we have to help Wil first. How do we cure a vampire bite?"

"Sunlight?"

"We'll open her drapes. But what if that's not enough?"

Theo snapped her fingers. "Garlic!" She pulled her bottle of garlic salt out of her pocket. "Thank you, Quincy!"

"Perfect!" Alexander said. "I think they also use holy water in the movies?"

"That's confusing," Theo said. "What makes water holy? And besides, who's to say the original instruction was holy, not holey? Maybe you're supposed to have water with holes in it. So, carbonated, I guess."

"Or just 'wholly water,' so, like, only water and nothing else." Alexander filled a glass to the brim with water and only water. They'd save Wil, and then he'd convince Wil and Theo to leave. It was one thing to stay overnight in a water park where people were disappearing in order to find them. It was another to stay overnight in a caspatle filled with vampires.

Peering out into the hallway, Theo gestured for Alexander to follow her. They darted through the eerily silent caspatle. The kids were with Quincy, and the grown-ups were with the Count. At least they'd be safe if they were with him. He didn't seem to be on the same team as Mina and Lucy.

"Maybe that's why the Count assigned all the kids to Quincy. To keep Mina away from us," Theo said.

"Maybe." Alexander unlocked Wil's door, careful not to spill his water, and they crept inside. The drapes were pulled tightly shut, the entire space as dim as a haunted graveyard at twilight. Wil was still cocooned in her blankets, not even her face visible.

"You do the drapes; I'll garlic her," Theo whispered.

"Are we sure about this?" Alexander had never considered what it might take to save a teenage sister from undead existence. Were they making the right choice?

"It has to be done," Theo said, her voice solemn but determined. No evil vampires were taking her sister away. "We do it on the count of three."

Alexander nodded. He took the drapes firmly in hand, watching over his shoulder. "One . . ." Theo unscrewed the lid to the garlic salt.

"Two . . . ," Alexander whispered, bracing himself as

though he were at the start of a race and didn't know what the finish line would bring.

"Three!"

Alexander flung open the drapes. Wil sat up, the blankets falling away from her face as she blinked bleary red eyes at them.

"Yaaaargh!" Theo shouted, and threw the whole bottle of garlic salt.

Wil screamed, clawing at her face.

Had they just saved their sister . . . *or destroyed her?*

CHAPTER
TWENTY-NINE

Wil screaming scared Alexander, so he started screaming, which made Theo scream, too. But they both stopped before Wil did.

"I'm going to destroy you twerps!" she sputtered.

"Because you're a vampire?" Alexander asked, terrified. The light from the window only seemed to make her mad, and the garlic wasn't doing anything besides making her sneeze and her eyes water.

"Because you woke me up by throwing garlic salt in my face! It really stings!"

Alexander held out the glass of water. Wil grabbed it and dumped it on her face, blinking away the salt that had gotten in her eyes. "What's wrong with you?"

Theo folded her arms, mimicking her mother's you're-in-trouble-and-I-mean-business pose. "We know you got bitten! You're turning into a vampire, but we won't let it happen!"

"Bitten by what?" Wil asked.

"A vampire bat, probably." Alexander sat on the edge of the bed. He pointed to the window. "We saw one hanging out there. We should have done more to protect you. I'm so, so sorry."

"I didn't get bitten by anything!"

Alexander shook his head. It wasn't like Wil to lie. It was probably the vampire powers, overtaking her. "We saw the bite marks on your neck."

If Wil wasn't already covered in water and garlic salt, maybe they would have seen the angry flush to her face that indicated she was both annoyed and embarrassed but hardly ready to suck out anyone's blood.

Wil slapped her hand over her neck. "Right there?" she asked.

Theo nodded. "Don't worry. We'll figure out a way to save you. I promise."

Wil flopped back onto her pillow, then pulled it over her face and screamed into it before slowly pulling it away. Theo and Alexander could tell she was working very, very hard to be calm. Even as a vampire, Wil was a good older sister. They should have appreciated her more while she was still human.

"Those," Wil said, her teeth clenched, "are"—she sat up and stared in exasperation at the ceiling—"*zits.*"

"What?" Theo asked.

"Huh?" Alexander echoed.

"They're zits, you little twerps! Thanks for noticing! It's been hard to keep up my skin care routine with all this upheaval, okay? And I've been really stressed out!"

"But you—you're sleeping during the day, and you weren't in your room in the middle of the night, and you don't want the light, and . . ." Alexander trailed off.

Wil gestured to Rodrigo. "Better Wi-Fi signal at night because no one else is using it then. I've been up, working."

"Working on what? It's *summer.*" If Theo were a vampire, she was sure she'd have lots of convenient reasons why she was acting all vampiric. Actually, she'd be a fantastic vampire. Probably the best one. Not that it was a competition, but if it were, Theo was sure she'd win.

"Never mind," Wil muttered. "You don't need to worry about it, okay? And you don't need to worry about vampires, either. They're not real. What have you two been doing, anyway? You've gone off the deep end."

"No, we're not at the water park anymore. There is no deep end." Alexander shook his head. "Theo did go off a cliff, though."

"You *what?*"

"It's a long story." Theo waved dismissively.

Wil rubbed her face, wiping away the leftover garlic goo. "Right. Well. Be more careful. No more cliffs. And don't worry about me. I promise I can take care of myself. If anything, I should be taking care of you two. It sounds like you need it more." Her phone chimed, and she looked down, lost in Rodrigo again.

"Right. Well, we're going to go carve some wooden stakes," Theo said.

"And find the nearest villagers with pitchforks and torches," Alexander added.

"Maybe grow bat wings and fangs while we're at it."

"Right, good, have fun," Wil said, waving them away.

Alexander followed Theo into the hall. "Well?" he asked. "What do you think?"

"If I were a vampire, I'd deny that I was one."

"No, you wouldn't," Alexander said. "You'd brag about it to everyone."

Theo laughed. "Yeah, that's true. And Wil's pretty

honest. Or at least, she used to be." Theo glared at the door. Why wasn't Wil telling them what she was really up to? What did she mean she was *working*?

"I don't think she's a vampire." Alexander was certain of that, or at least as certain as he could be. Which meant their sister was safe. They had done the cautious thing and taken care of her first. Which he supposed meant they could make a brave choice now. After all, it was one thing to run away and save yourself. It was another to run away and save yourself, leaving behind friends like Quincy and Eris and the Js and Ren. Well, Ren wasn't really a friend. But even he didn't deserve to be vampified. And neither did the two sticky toddlers. Being vampires was the only way they could possibly be any scarier or worse than they already were.

"Let's read the vampire book," Alexander said, "and see if it gives us any clues about how to deal with them."

As they went down the hall, a tiny figure dropped from the ceiling. Lucy stood there, wearing a white night-gown. Her golden hair almost seemed to float around her face, and her big, dark eyes stared unblinking at them. She was as pale as winter snow, except her lips, which were even redder than the Count's. She flicked Alexander's yo-yo up and down, then swung it in a wide circle so they couldn't get by. They turned to run in the other direction, only to find that way blocked by Mina.

"We need to talk," Mina said, folding her arms.

"We know your secrets!" Alexander held up the book as proof.

"You figured it out, then," Mina said, her shoulders dropping. She didn't look angry, or triumphant, or evil. She just looked sad. "It's all over, I guess. I tried so hard to take care of everything myself. I'm sorry, Lucy."

Alexander wondered if this was a trick. He puffed out his chest, determined not to fall for it, even if he did feel bad for Mina and want her to be happy again. "Yes," he said, trying to sound confident. "We know you're vampires."

"Huh?" Mina said at the same time Lucy let out a giggle behind them.

"And we know what your sixth-favorite animal is!" Theo shouted, triumphant. But when she turned, Lucy had disappeared. "It's bats!" Theo yelled.

Lucy's disappointed voice drifted from the darkness above them. "No, it's not."

Theo tugged on her hair in frustration. "Ocelots! Pangolins! Manta rays! Tortoises!" But Lucy was gone. Probably turned into a bat or mist or something annoying like that.

"Please give me the book," Mina said, holding out her hand. Afraid of what she might do if he didn't, Alexander gave it to her. "It's time you learned everything." Mina cracked the book open, and Alexander and Theo held their breath.

CHAPTER
THIRTY

There's an old saying that goes, *You can't judge a book by its cover,* about not deciding what people are like based only on their looks. And, for the most part, it's true. Maybe you meet a man who looks like a turkey vulture but ends up being genuinely kind and concerned for the safety of children and not at all like a carrion bird looking for carcasses to pick clean. Or maybe you meet a beautiful teenager named Mina who you want to trust because she's so sweet but then it turns out she might be a vampire, so you really should hold judgment until you know her better and not let your blooming crush determine whether or not you follow her down a dark stairway into a cave full of bats.

When it comes to books, though, it's pretty safe to judge them by their covers. Whole teams of talented, artistic people very carefully design covers meant to be judged. *Please!* those covers scream from the shelves. *Judge me as something you want to read! Judge me as your favorite!* Usually actual book covers, and their titles, tell you a lot of what you need to know about a book.

In the case of *The Care and Keeping of Vampir—*, though, the cover did not, in fact, tell the story. Or at least, the whole story.

Mina opened the book to the title page and held it out to Theo and Alexander.

"*The Care and Keeping of Vampire . . . Bats?*" Alexander read. "This is a book about how to help a vampire bat colony thrive." He had more questions than he had before.

"So your bats are vampires, too! I knew it!" Theo shouted. Then she paused, her triumph slightly deflating. She watched a lot of nature documentaries with her dad. Her favorite was called *Fangs, Fur, and Fins* and was all about ranking which animals would win in theoretical fights. She had never seen vampire bats featured because they weren't fighters. "Wait. Aren't vampire bats, like, not at all threats to humans?"

Mina nodded. "They're gentle, sweet creatures who need very little blood to survive and don't harm the animals they take it from, and who take care of each other."

"So, in the cave . . . ," Theo prodded.

"That's our colony." Mina smiled, her face warming with affection. "My great-great-grandmother brought them from South America long ago. My family's been caring for and studying them ever since. And keeping them secret. There's a lot of prejudice against bats, particularly of the vampire variety. People don't understand that a scary name doesn't necessarily mean a scary thing," said Mina Blood to Alexander and Theo Sinister-Winterbottom.

"You wanted to keep them secret because you were worried people would be scared of them?" Alexander asked.

"Well, that's part of it. But the truth is . . ." Mina wrung her hands. "Well, the truth is, I'm keeping them a secret from the Count. I know technically everything on the Sanguine Spa grounds belongs to him, but they're the last thing I have left of my parents. I just couldn't turn over their research to him. I don't know what he'll do with it, or how he'll treat the bats. He's already changed the spa so much, and I couldn't bear it if he took over the lab, too."

"Wait, the lab?" Theo was intrigued. "Like, a secret laboratory?"

"Exactly like that. You see, in addition to running the Sanguine Spa, my parents were doctors. Vampire bats have a special anticlotting property to their saliva. It has the potential to help people with certain blood disorders. People like Lucy."

"Lucy's a person?" Theo asked, genuinely shocked.

Mina laughed. "Of course she is."

"But—she appears and disappears and sometimes is only a disembodied voice, and she climbs straight up the walls!"

"Well, she's a very coordinated person. And she knows the hotel better than anyone. She has all sorts of tricks for getting around. You see, Lucy's allergic to sunlight."

Theo had often wished to be allergic to certain things—eggplant, for one, which her mother insisted was a good substitution for meat in food, which Theo really, really did not agree with, but also homework, which Theo was pretty certain she *was* allergic to, because every time she tried to sit down to do it she got twitchy and uncomfortable and had to move around—but sunlight was definitely not something Theo had ever wished she could avoid because of allergies. "That's bad," Theo said.

"It is," Mina agreed. "And it means she has to be watched very carefully, because she doesn't always make the safest choices."

"All those times you were yelling at the ceiling!"

"Yes." Mina sighed heavily. "I knew without my parents, they wouldn't let me keep Lucy. But I knew no one else could take care of her like I can. So I lied to the Count and said she was gone. And Lucy agreed to stay hidden so no one would know she was still here. But she didn't do a great job. She gets lonely, and apparently she likes you two."

"We're very likable," Theo said, nodding.

"Anyway, in addition to her light allergy, she also has blood . . . issues. And there was reason to hope with the vampire bat colony and my parents' research. They believed they could eventually cure Lucy of her problems. So I've taken up their work. Studied all their notes, learned what I needed. But the Count keeps me so busy with the spa that between work and looking out for Lucy, I barely have time for the bats. I miss them so much!"

"Are they like pets?" Theo wanted a dog, or a cat, or a

Komodo dragon. She hadn't ever considered having a bat as a pet.

"No, we only observe and make sure they're healthy. They're such delicate, sensitive creatures. And kind! They help each other. They adopt baby bats if they're orphaned. Or if one bat doesn't find food for the night, the others will share so it doesn't die. So they can all stay *together.*" Mina's eyes filled with tears.

Alexander and Theo never thought they'd relate so much to fuzzy flying mice that drank blood to survive, but they couldn't help but be touched by this information. "I would share my blood with you," Theo said, nudging Alexander.

"Gross. But same."

"Are you sure there aren't any vampires, though?" Theo asked. "We looked in the spa, and there were those red vials, and all the parents seemed unconscious."

Mina shook her head. "I can confidently say it's not vampires, but also, I don't really understand what's happening in the spa. The Count is obsessed with those smoothies, and he won't tell me what's in them. Speaking of the Count, we'd better put this book back. I don't want him to find out about the bats, just like I don't want him to find out about Lucy." She paused. "I'm sorry I'm asking you to keep secrets that aren't even yours. I understand if you don't want to."

"We want to!" Alexander blurted, relieved that he had correctly judged Mina by her cover. And also relieved that it looked like there were not, in fact, scary vampires. Only fuzzy flying nonthreatening vampires and strange little girls. But mostly relieved that Mina wasn't evil and he could keep feeling these confusing flutters for her.

They followed Mina into the library, where she reverently replaced the book on the shelf.

Theo climbed onto the ladder because she couldn't *not* be on the ladder if she was in this library. "So what were Quincy and the Count having us search for, if there aren't any vampires?"

"Oh no." Mina put her hands over her mouth.

Alexander realized it at the same time. "That's what he's using the spa for. He's already experimenting with the parents. He just needs your parents' research and the laboratory! But he doesn't know where they are."

Mina nodded. "I think you're right. What are we going to do?"

"We tell the grown-ups they're being medically experimented on instead of being pampered like they're paying for." Theo shrugged. Seemed obvious to her. "Oh, look!

Speaking of vampires, here's Dracula himself!" Laughing, Theo grabbed the spine of *Dracula*, Bram Stoker's classic vampire novel, and tugged on it.

But instead of the book coming off the shelf, the whole shelf swung open.

CHAPTER
THIRTY-ONE

"Is that a secret library? *Inside* the library? A library within a library!?" Alexander asked. Much like Theo had never dared to dream of a library with built-in rolling ladders for entertainment, Alexander had never dreamed that libraries could be even more libraryish than they already were.

Mina took a step inside, eyes wide with wonder. "I didn't know this room existed!"

"We find a lot of hidden rooms lately. We always think they're storage, but they never are." Theo shrugged. She wasn't that excited about the hidden library. It didn't have any ladders, rolling or otherwise. There was one long table, with an ornate lamp in the center. The room had no windows and no other doors. Almost like it was meant to be unfindable, or at least meant to keep the contents protected from anything that might damage them, like sunlight.

Mina stepped forward and pulled the chain on the lamp. It was decorated with a delicate stained-glass pattern of bats. The bats formed a border around the edge of the lampshade. Once the light shone out from the bats and the blood-red glass, the intrepid explorers saw that the table had several books on it. They were large, ornate, and bound with thick, heavy leather. And . . . *locked.*

"Who locks a book?" Theo demanded. She had had just about enough of locks lately. She grabbed the lasso out of her pocket and began twirling it, determined to master at least one skill. How did one go about learning lockpicking? Maybe there was a book in the regular library about it.

"Sinister," Alexander whispered.

"Yeah!" Theo agreed. "It *is* sinister to lock a book! What do they think the pages are going to do, run away?"

"No," Alexander said, pointing to the cover of the first locked book. Etched into the leather and filled with delicate gold was the name *SINISTER.*

239

Theo frowned. "That's our name. Or at least, Mom's name. Aunt Saffronia's, too."

"*Blood*," Mina said, running her fingers along the cover of another one of the books. "Why would they have a book with our name on it and lock it?" All the books on the table were locked, not just the Blood and Sinister books.

"That one says *Widow* on the cover!" Theo said, going around the table, reading the covers. They were all single words, and she suspected they were all names. "That's Edgar's last name. Why would they have a book about the family running the water park?"

"Why would they have a book about us?" Alexander asked.

"Why would they have a standing reservation for Sinisters at the spa?"

"Why . . . ?" Alexander trailed off. "Well, I can't think of any other whys. Those whys are big enough." He leaned closer to the Sinister book. Tiny letters were etched in the metal around the lock, but they were too small for him to read. Carefully attached to the spine of the book was exactly what he needed: a magnifying glass. It was a beautiful object, with an ornate brass handle and perfectly clear glass. Alexander detached it from the book, then held it up to his eye. Theo laughed. It made one of Alexander's eyes twice as big as the other. Even his irises had freckles on them, the brown spotted with green.

"Eye see you," Theo said.

"Eye know," Alexander answered. "Do you see any keys, though?"

Mina was searching under the table and on all the shelves, while Theo aggressively shook the Widow book to see if anything fell out. Ideally a key.

"Oh!" Alexander lowered the magnifying glass to read the words etched into the lock. Maybe they would tell him how to open it. But before he could make them out, they were interrupted.

"If I'm correct," a voice outside said, "then there's a library within the library, and—" Wil burst in. Her eyes widened in shock to see her siblings and Mina already in the library within the library. She lowered Rodrigo and ended the call she was on. "How did you— *The Sinister Book?*" Wil asked, and the way she said it, with intense focus and recognition, made Theo and Alexander suspect she was saying each word with a capital letter, and that she somehow already knew the book existed.

If Alexander and Theo hadn't already been suspicious that something was up with Wil, they definitely were now, because she put Rodrigo in her pocket.

She put.

Rodrigo.

In.

Her.

Pocket.

Wil rushed past them, looking at each of the books, running her fingers over the covers as she whispered the names to herself. Alexander put the magnifying glass in his own pocket, not wanting it to get scratched on the table.

"Blood, Widow, Hyde, Siren, Stein, Graves. And Sinister. They're all here," Wil said. "All of them! Finally." She laughed, shaking her head with relief.

"How do you know about the books?" Mina asked. "I didn't even know they were here."

"I'll tell you later, when we have time." Wil held out her hand. "Give me the keys. I need to open this one."

"I don't have them," Mina said.

Wil let out an enraged growl. "Now I have the books but not the keys! It's always something. Okay. If you were a missing key, where would you be?"

"Lucy!" Mina snapped her fingers. "She finds everything that's lost. Actually, she's usually the one who takes things in the first place. But if we—"

"You told her," a voice, formerly friendly and now utterly betrayed, said.

Mina, Theo, and Alexander whipped around. Quincy was standing in the doorway to the library. Her eyes were pooling with tears. "I told you not to tell Mina you were looking for something. I told you it was important. I thought we were friends."

"We were," Alexander said.

"We are," Theo added. "But there's so much you don't know."

"No," Quincy said, shaking her head. "There's so much *you* don't know. And I was trying to help you, to protect you, but . . . I'm sorry." She stepped to the side. Behind her appeared the Count, sweeping into the room like the world's most unwelcome Roomba, devouring that last tiny Lego piece most needed to finish a project.

"What have we here? Mina, you know better than to snoop," the Count sneered. "And you two! You Swinterbottom children!"

"Actually, it's—" Alexander started, but the Count cut him off.

"You clearly need more group participation time. I—" His phone rang, and he held up one long, bony finger with a too-long fingernail. His pale face got even paler as he answered. "Yes, hello? . . . I understand. I'm working on it. I . . . No, I told you, they never checked in. It's my hotel after all! I would certainly notice if three unaccompanied children named Sinister checked in. The only unaccompanied children are Quincy and the Swinterbottoms. . . . Yes, Swinterbottoms. . . . No, I know it's a very strange name. . . . Yes, we can switch to video."

He held the phone out. A deep, unpleasant voice that seemed oddly familiar said, "Do the Swinterbottom children look like this?" Alexander and Theo couldn't see what the person on the other line was doing, but they had a sinking feeling in their stomachs. Perhaps he was gesturing wildly around his head, to demonstrate Theo's Albert Einstein hair. Or perhaps he was making an extremely worried expression, to demonstrate how Alexander often looked. Or perhaps he was holding up his own phone, eyes glued to it to demonstrate Wil's constant pose. Little did they know the man was, in fact, holding up detailed drawings of the Sinister-Winterbottom children.

"Yes! That's them."

"Keep them on hand. I'll be there soon." The call ended.

"You can't keep us here," Wil said, standing straight and glaring defiantly. She had the Sinister book clutched to her chest like a shield.

"Actually, I can." The Count smiled with all his many, many unpleasant teeth. "There's no one here to stick up for you, no one here in charge of you, no one here to leave me a bad rating on Gulp. Which means *I'm* in control of you, and I have been since the moment you checked in. Which means if I decide to lock you in here for your own good, there's nothing anyone can do about it." He grabbed Mina, spinning her into the main library, and slammed the secret door shut.

The Sinister-Winterbottoms were trapped.

CHAPTER
THIRTY-TWO

"This is Mom and Dad's fault." Theo sat at the table, sinking low in her seat. She had been all over the wall, but there was no way she could find to open the door from this side. They were making a bad habit of being trapped in secret rooms.

"What are we even doing here?" Alexander leaned glumly against the table. It was a *family* spa, a *family* vacation, and because they weren't here as a whole family, they were at the mercy of a very mean man. Their mother's letter had been wrong. Being brave or cautious didn't matter. Nothing did. This whole summer was one big mess. And Alexander hated messes.

"Where are the keys to these books?" Wil desperately clawed at the locks, trying to pry them open.

Alexander shifted, and his pocket clanked against the counter, reminding him that it wasn't empty. He pulled out the magnifying glass. Why had this been attached to the Sinister book? On the bottom of the magnifying glass, emblazoned on the brass handle, he found *A.S.* His own initials. Was it a coincidence?

"What do you use magnifying glasses for?" he mused quietly to himself.

"To look closer at things." Theo was bonking her head against the table. Her bees were buzzing wildly, hating being trapped as much as she did.

"Do you remember," Alexander said, his own mind whirring, "what Aunt Saffronia said to us, after she picked us up from Fathoms of Fun? We thought she wanted us to find Mr. Widow and solve the mystery of what happened to him. But it turned out she just wanted you to find that timer."

Theo pulled the timer from under her shirt and stared down at it. "Yeah. That was weird. Hey, did I tell you it has my initials on it?"

"*What?*" Alexander hurried over to Theo's side. Sure

enough, in scrolling letters on the back, a perfect match to the letters on Alexander's object, were the initials *T.S.*

Alexander held out the magnifying glass and showed Theo. "Do you think this is what she wanted us to find? She told us we needed to be able to look closer."

"You found that attached to the Sinister book?" Wil asked. She peered at it. "But there's no way to use it to open the book." She shook her head, sitting down and getting back to work on trying to undo the lock.

Theo stared at the initials, aghast. She loved the word *aghast*. It was like *surprised*, but in a ghastly way. She didn't get to feel aghast very often, but she knew exactly how she felt now and how to describe it, which was a nice change. "Is Aunt Saffronia sending us on these weird vacations to *steal* things for her?" Theo couldn't believe it. Aunt Saffronia had taken in three children to run an untraceable theft ring! If it weren't illegal and wrong, it would be downright cool. Theo could already imagine herself as a top-notch cat burglar, using her new lasso skills to scale buildings, and her soon-to-be-new lockpicking skills to crack even the most secure safes.

"But you didn't steal that," Alexander reminded her. "Edgar gave it to you. And I'm not taking this."

"I'll bet Mina would let you have it. She didn't even know it was in there. And it was attached to the Sinister book, not the Blood book. It literally had our names on it."

"Yeah, I guess." Alexander was tired. He was tired of running around the hotel, being yelled at both directly and indirectly. He was tired of worrying about vampires, and Wil, and Vampire Wil. He was tired of having to figure things out without a parent. He was tired of wondering what Aunt Saffronia really wanted from them, and why their parents left them with such a weird, irresponsible, possibly theft-prone relative.

The Count was right. No one here was looking out for them. No one would stick up for them. They were on their own, and he wanted to go home.

"Wil, can I use your phone?"

It was a testament to just how bleak things were, how mysterious, how bizarre, that Wil simply handed Rodrigo over, all her attention on trying to open the book. Alexander dialed Aunt Saffronia's number—easy to remember because it was like a date—and waited as it rang and rang and then was claimed by that strange, overwhelming static.

"Yes?" Aunt Saffronia said.

"What if I found what you wanted me to find? Would you come pick us up before the week is over?"

"If you've found what we need—if we can look closer now—then there is no reason for you to stay at the Sanguine Spa. Indeed, it might even be perilous. We must put your safety first. It's what your mother would want."

Since when did Aunt Saffronia put their safety first? She'd let them stay overnight at a water park being run by criminals! She dropped them off at this spa without even walking in, or checking the schedule, or knowing whether they would be looked after. Which they certainly were not being. They were definitely being *watched*, but that was very different.

Alexander lowered the phone. "She'll come get us," he said to Theo and Wil. The Count couldn't keep them locked up when their guardian was there.

"Do you have it?" Aunt Saffronia said, her distant voice becoming urgent and somehow sounding closer. "We must hurry! On to the next!"

"But," Theo said, now standing next to Alexander with her head pressed against the phone, too. "We have friends here. Friends who might still need our help." Because there was no denying that Mina needed help. The

Count had her, and whoever was coming didn't sound like someone who would have Mina's and Lucy's and the bats' best interests at heart.

"If you have what we need," Aunt Saffronia said, her voice as clear as if she were in the next room now, "then it doesn't matter. I'll be there at once."

"Listen to Aunt Saffronia," Alexander whispered.

"Except when you shouldn't." Theo reminded Alexander of the next part of the letter. They considered it together. They could get out of this weird, creepy caspatle. They could leave it all behind. They could ditch the Count and never have to see him again.

Or they could stay, and see if there was some way they could really help Mina, who was a good person and deserved to be helped. And who was all on her own. Without parents to stick up for her, or to navigate the weirdness of the world so she could just be a carefree teenager.

Theo and Alexander looked at Wil. "Your call," she said. "As long as we have these books."

"*Except when we shouldn't,*" Alexander whispered, nodding. Theo smiled grimly. They were in agreement. Maybe they had found what Aunt Saffronia needed. Maybe she was right, and they should put themselves first and leave. But if they had a chance to help someone who needed help, they knew their parents would want them to do it.

"Haven't found it yet," Theo chirped, and Alexander was grateful that he wasn't the one who had to lie. But it wasn't exactly a lie, was it? They didn't know for sure that the magnifying glass was what Aunt Saffronia wanted. After all, it was such a random object. Why would she need it?

"I see," Aunt Saffronia said, her voice fading like she was being tugged down a tunnel, farther and farther from them. "Or rather, I don't. I see so little, until I'm summoned. Very well. Until it is time, be careful. There are those who have sinister purposes against our Sinister purposes, and I fear they are getting closer. Watch each other's necks, dear children."

"Do you mean because of vampires?" Theo asked at the same time Alexander said, "There aren't any vampires."

"Of course," Aunt Saffronia said.

"Wait," Alexander said. "Do you mean of course because of vampires, or of course there aren't any?"

The line went dead.

Theo handed Rodrigo back to Wil. "Well, we're staying. And that means we have to figure out a way to escape from this room."

"But we can't open it from this side." Alexander wished he could speak with whoever was making these secret doors that only opened from the outside. It was a very big design flaw. "We're trapped."

"Who do we know who gets around the entire cas-patle without ever seeming to use a door?" Theo asked, pointing upward. A little wooden yo-yo was dangling from the darkest corner where the ceiling met the wall behind a beam. Theo beamed triumphantly. "Lucy's not turning into mist. She's using *secret passageways*. And we will, too."

CHAPTER
THIRTY-THREE

It was tricky figuring out how to get to the corner of the ceiling, but Theo was up for the challenge. She shoved the table into the corner, then balanced a chair on top of it, climbing precariously.

"I was right!" she shouted, looking past the yo-yo. "There's a little hole here." She paused, looking down at Alexander and Wil. "A very little hole. I don't think Wil can fit."

Wil nodded. "Fine by me. I don't like tight spaces anyway. I'll stay here and work on the books. You two twerps can squeeze through, find a way out, and then get the door open from the other side. Teamwork."

"We haven't been much of a team lately," Alexander said.

Wil tugged on one of her braids. "I know. I'm sorry. I've just—I've been trying to make sure you two can have a normal summer."

Theo laughed, crouched in the corner of a ceiling, about to enter a dark hole to navigate secret passageways, escape the notice of a mean Count, and save a bunch of vampire bats from discovery. "I don't think that's going to happen."

"You're right. And you two are smarter and more capable than I give you credit for. After all, you found the secret library before I did!"

"How did you know to look for it?" Alexander asked.

"Escape first, explanations after." Wil pointed to the hole.

Theo held out a hand and helped poor Alexander make his shaky, terrified way up.

Wil sat on the floor with the Sinister book in her lap. "Take your time. I'm not going anywhere."

"Ha, ha," Theo said. Then she disappeared. Alexander followed, really, really wishing his part of this plan had been to hang out with books rather than squeeze through darkness.

Theo went confidently in one direction. Then she bumped straight into a wall. It was narrow and dark, and she couldn't see where she was going. Having a great sense of direction didn't help much when she couldn't see anything and had no idea what the layout of the passages was.

"Back up," she said. Alexander did his best. But after a few minutes, it was clear they weren't any closer to getting Wil out of the library, and they weren't any closer to getting themselves out of this dusty, claustrophobic nightmare.

There was a little laugh somewhere nearby.

"Lucy?" Theo called.

The laugh continued.

"Please," Alexander said. "We want to help you and Mina. We want to keep the bats and the lab safe. And we also want to get our sister free and figure out what's in those books in the secret library. There's a book in there for your family, too. Maybe your parents left instructions or letters in there." He couldn't help but hope maybe *his* parents had. The Sinister book seemed to call to him with promises of answers. If not answers for why his parents left them the whole summer, at least a connection to their family. Something he could take along into the unknown summer still stretching long and hot and confusing in front of them. A book he could hold, could learn from.

Alexander's yo-yo reappeared out of nowhere, coated in glow-in-the-dark nail polish. It began sliding away. "Follow that yo-yo!" Theo cried.

They could only crawl, and they had to crawl fast to keep up with Lucy's trail. But once they knew where to go, it was obvious there was, in fact, a pattern. These weren't air ducts. They had been designed to be moved through. But for what purpose?

"No light," Lucy said chipperly from somewhere ahead of them. It was true. The tunnels were really, *really* dark. Because of the movement of cold air around them, Theo could tell there were branching tunnels every few feet. They probably led to every part of the caspatle. And they let someone small—like Lucy—get around without ever going in the light, or setting foot outside.

And they also made it so someone like Theo or Alexander would get impossibly lost without a guide.

Lucy led them to a wall that had rungs bolted in place. There was a hint of light coming in through cracks in the stones, so at least Theo and Alexander could see what they were doing as they climbed up to the next floor of the caspatle, then along another crawling tunnel, around several corners, and finally to a dead end.

"Um," Alexander said, staring at the bottoms of Theo's worn sneakers. "Is there a reason we stopped? Was there a cave-in? Are we stuck?" He started backing up, terrified. But then light flooded in. Lucy hopped out of the wooden panel she had slid open to create a door. Theo followed, and then Alexander gratefully escaped from the secret passages.

"It's a closet," Theo said, looking at beautiful jewel-toned coats and several dramatic velvet capes. Lucy rubbed her face against one of the capes.

"It's your parents' closet." Alexander recognized one of the fancy dresses, and one of the spooky cloaks. Plus, there was a cane there, with the silver wolf-dragon head. The same cane Mr. Blood had held in his portrait. "The paintings," Alexander said. "*You* change them." Someone really *was* trying to tell him something with the paintings. Or rather, just trying to remind herself of her own story, her own family.

Lucy nodded, tugging down a deep purple cape and wrapping herself in it like a blanket.

Theo put an arm around the strange little girl and

turned to Alexander. "Let's get out of this closet. From here we can—"

"I told you, I'm working on it!" the Count said, his voice much closer than they wanted it to be. But even worse was the voice that answered it. Now that it wasn't through a phone, they knew exactly who it belonged to. It was a deep voice. A familiar voice. A voice whose preferred type of leftover pizza in the fridge was an empty box left to trick someone else into hoping that they would find something good inside, only to be disappointed.

A voice that belonged to a man with small, mean eyes and a large, mean mustache.

"Edgaren't?" Theo and Alexander whispered to each other.

CHAPTER
THIRTY-FOUR

I t *couldn't* be Edgaren't. They had last seen that villain running into the woods after his Fathoms of Fun scheme had failed. What would he be doing here? There was no connection between the two vacation destinations, no reason for him to—

"The books," Alexander whispered. One of the locked books in the hidden library had the name Widow on it. That was the name of the family that ran the water park. Maybe Edgaren't was still trying to get his hands on the land and the wealth of oil underneath it.

Edgaren't sounded angry as he continued arguing

with the Count. "You've had plenty of time. Why haven't you found it yet?"

The Count sounded whiny. "It's a huge hotel! And the Bloods kept a lot of secrets from me! I need a little more time, or several more children."

"Why do you need children?"

"Oh, child labor is the best kind of labor! Everyone knows that. You don't have to pay them; you tell them they're each looking for something secret and they can't tell anyone else. They're already nosy little pests so they love that, and best of all, they're small enough to fit into unexpected places."

The three children hiding in an unexpected closet held their breath.

"I'm almost there, Van Helsing," the Count continued. "I can feel it."

Theo and Alexander looked at each other with a frown. Who was Van Helsing?

"Van H.," Theo whispered, urgently. They had lugged his trunk up all on their own! She really should have thrown it down the stairs! "Edgaren't is Van H.!"

"And you're sure the three Sinister children are contained? They can't wriggle free and ruin everything?"

"I'm sure. I trapped them in a library. They'll be absolutely miserable—all children hate libraries."

"True. Take me to Mina, then. I'm sure she knows more than she's saying."

"Of course. But first, you simply must try one of my health smoothies. It will change your life."

As soon as they heard the door close, the three children collapsed onto the floor of the closet, sitting knee-to-knee-to-knee.

"What are we going to do?" Theo asked. She didn't have a plan for this.

"Maybe we should have left when Aunt Saffronia offered to pick us up. I don't want to deal with Edgaren't again." Alexander twisted his hands, imagining how much meaner Edgaren't's mustache must have gotten in the last few days.

"But if Edgaren't is here, that means things are worse than we thought for Mina and the caspatle. Edgaren't almost got Fathoms of Fun away from the Widows. And he wants the Count to find something. He probably wants the bat laboratory. Medical research can be worth a lot of money!"

Alexander sighed. "This was all simpler when it was

about vampires." He paused. "*That's* a sentence I never thought I'd say."

"If only we could unlock this mystery." Theo grabbed tufts of her hair like she did sometimes when the bees got too loud and she had to do something with her hands.

At the word *unlock*, Lucy perked up. She gestured for them to follow and climbed back into the crawl space. Theo eagerly followed, and Alexander reluctantly followed. It said a lot about Edgaren't that Alexander preferred the near pitch-black confines of these secret passages to the risk of accidentally running into that mean mustache in the halls.

"How can she see anything in here?" Alexander whispered. In spite of the occasional wall cracks letting in slivers of light, there was no way Alexander could have found his way anywhere in these crawl spaces.

Theo, too, had been wondering the same thing. Lucy navigated with ease, turning corners, never pausing. "Maybe she has all the different paths memorized." But just as Theo said it, Lucy dropped out of sight, *gone*.

"Lucy!" Theo crawled forward as fast as she could. She looked down and saw nothing, only darkness. Then there was the hiss of a match and a candle flickered to life, revealing a cozy little space in the center of several intersecting tunnels. It could really only be described as a nest. It had books, pillows, paintings, shoes (but only the left ones), stacks of papers, one of Alexander's favorite shirts, one of Quincy's cowboy hats, a tube of Wil's best lip gloss, what looked like an entire drawer's worth of silverware, and keys.

Lots and lots of keys. So many keys.

Lucy gestured to them, that small secret smile lighting her face much like the candle lit the nest. Though Alexander was less afraid that the light of Lucy's small secret smile might accidentally catch all these very flammable objects on fire. Candles were *not* a safe lighting choice here.

"Steal a flashlight next, okay?" he said. "Please?"

Lucy nodded solemnly.

Alexander picked up the nearest piece of paper. It was in a familiar envelope, with even more familiar cursive on it. Lucy had taken the letter their mother left for them in his suitcase. He was almost tempted to leave it. He was, for the first time, mad at his parents instead of just worried and sad.

But he couldn't leave it behind. "This is mine," he said

softly, as kindly as he could. "You can keep the yo-yo, but I need this back." He put it in his pocket next to the magnifying glass.

Lucy kept her red lips firmly closed like she was holding a secret in her mouth, staring up at him with those big black eyes.

Theo was pawing through the keys. "I think we could unlock any door in the whole hotel!" She was so excited not to have locked doors. But a little disappointed she no longer had a compelling reason to become a master lockpick. It wouldn't deter her, though. Surely it was a skill that would come in handy for other reasons.

Alexander noticed several keys on a brass ring. They were small and ornate, exactly the right size to unlock . . .

"The books," he and Theo said at the same time.

The last time they faced him, Edgaren't had been looking for a book, too. The book of contracts and the deed to Fathoms of Fun. Maybe the instructions to find the bats or the details of the medical research were in the books in the hidden library. Or maybe he wasn't looking for the books at all. But Alexander and Theo were desperate to unlock their own book, and they knew Mina wanted hers as well.

"First things first," Alexander said, "we—"

"Find Edgaren't's car and slash his tires," Theo said, punching one fist into her other hand.

"But that would force him to stay, and we don't actually want him to."

"Oh, right." Sometimes the bees inside Theo wanted vengeance more than productive activity.

"But we *will* need to be brave," Alexander said, smiling at her. "After we're cautious. We've got to rescue Wil first. Lucy? While we go get Wil, can you beat Edgaren't and the Count to Mina and bring her to the library?"

Lucy nodded. She carefully added her mother's purple cape to the nest's pillow pile, then scrambled up another wall and gestured for them to follow. She let them out in the closet with the coffins. Or the big wooden boxes, which Alexander deliberately chose to think of them as. Then they crept carefully down the hall to the library door.

Theo hesitated. Edgaren't's/Heathcliff's/Van Helsing's room was right there, along with his trunk. She didn't have a key to his trunk, but she had shoved all the keys she could get into her pockets, so she was pretty sure she *did* have a key to his room.

"No," Alexander said, following her gaze. "Too risky."

Theo disagreed. She thought it was appropriately risky. But Wil needed to come first. Theo opened the door and ducked into the library without waiting. Alexander followed, closing the door behind him. The library was empty. Before Alexander could open the secret room, a chair against the wall seemed to move all on its own, until it was pushed far enough to allow Lucy and a dusty and astonished Mina to crawl out from the panel door behind it.

Just as they heard the rumble of a voice belonging to a large, mean mustache in the hall.

CHAPTER
THIRTY-FIVE

"Quick," Mina said. She opened the secret library and pushed Theo and Alexander in as Lucy retreated to the hole behind the chair. "They don't know you can get out!" Then the Sinister-Winterbottoms were once again locked up.

Almost as soon as the secret door had been closed, it swung open again. Theo and Alexander stood, panting, trying not to look guilty and hoping Edgaren't didn't notice the table pushed against the wall.

"I see you found my books," Edgaren't said. He reached out and snatched the Sinister book from Wil, then collected the rest from the table.

"These aren't yours!" Wil said. "That one has my name on it!"

"Well, *Swinterbottom*," the Count sneered, "I don't see that name anywhere. Besides which, the book is in my hotel. The hotel that I own. The hotel that became mine as soon as the Bloods were gone. The hotel that is absolutely my property from top to bottom, and no one can prove otherwise."

"He's right," Mina said sadly. "Everything here is his."

"And you would do well to remember that and give me what I want. No one is on your side. No one is going to help you, no matter what you've hidden. You know what I'm looking for, don't you?"

Mina nodded. She was going to lose her lab, and her bats, and it broke Alexander's heart.

"This isn't over," Wil said.

Edgaren't was smiling, which normally was a friendly expression, but behind his large, mean mustache, it was as friendly as a swarm of wasps. "No, but it will be soon. You three wait right here, safe and sound, until I come to collect you. Promise me you'll wait." His smile got bigger and meaner.

"No!" Theo said.

"Promise me you'll wait, or I'll burn this book." He held out the Sinister book. Wil let out a hiss of breath.

Alexander had never gone back on a promise before— not ever, not for anything. Thinking about a promise to Edgaren't made something inside Alexander break. But instead of feeling shattered, the broken thing seemed to let in a cool rush of calm. If the rules were made by people who didn't care about rules, who were only trying to hurt others, then *Alexander didn't have to follow them.*

And a promise to a liar was no sort of promise at all.

"I promise," Alexander said. "Besides, the Count is right. Mina, you shouldn't have tried to keep it from him. Everything here is legally the Count's, and you should take him to it."

Mina looked at Alexander in shock, her eyes brimming with tears. Theo made an outraged noise, but Alexander ignored both things, much as he wanted to apologize. He kept talking. "Make sure Mina takes you the short way, through the hedge maze. It takes exactly thirty minutes and leads you directly to the trail. You'll never find it otherwise."

Mina's expression froze, her lips twitching. Then she cleared her throat, scowling, as she pulled out her watch and looked at the time so she'd know exactly when her thirty minutes were up. "How could you tell them about the shortcut?"

"It's the right thing to do," Alexander said, trying his absolute hardest not to smile at her. He had bought them half an hour.

"Let's go." Edgaren't slammed the secret door shut.

"Why did you do that?" Wil asked, turning to Alexander.

"Because," he said, "we're going to beat them. Start your timer, Theo! We have thirty minutes."

"To do what?" she asked, clicking the button on top of her timer, then tucking it back under her shirt again.

"Oh," Alexander said, biting his lip. "I . . . don't actually know."

CHAPTER

THIRTY-SIX

Wil slumped against the table, then put her head down on her arms. Her hand slipped into her pocket, and she pulled out Rodrigo, holding it for comfort.

"I had it," she whispered. "And now it's gone."

"It's not fair!" Theo shrieked, kicking the door. "We can get out, sure, but then what? They still win! We need help! Where are our parents?" Theo breathed hard, and suddenly her anger had somehow turned to tears. She wiped furiously at them, then turned around, looking at Alexander. "Where are they?" she repeated, lost, because without their parents, they really were just kids. They couldn't help Mina, or themselves, or anyone. And no one was going to help them, because the people who should—their parents, their aunt—weren't here.

"Theo," Alexander said, taking her hand. He could tell she was freaking out. What did their mom do when that happened? He pulled Theo close and squeezed her, putting exactly the right amount of pressure on her so she could feel her whole body come back to a sense of who and where and what she was.

Theo took a few deep breaths. Alexander's hug helped her get control back. If she was filled with bees, well, fine. Bees were smart, bees were good workers, and bees had hives. She sent them back into their hives to get to work and stop swarming her brain. "I'm okay now. What do we do?"

"Be cautious, *check*. Be brave, *check*. What else can we try?" Alexander said.

"Listen to Aunt Saffronia, except when you shouldn't?" Theo shrugged. "Maybe we should have. Maybe when we called her, we should have had her come and pick us up. Sometimes you really do need a grown-up. Even a weird, useless one."

"That's it!" Alexander shouted.

"What's it?"

"Wil, use your phone!" Alexander pointed emphatically at Rodrigo.

"And do what?" Wil asked, finally lifting her head.

"Look up the phone numbers of the grown-ups here. The parents."

"I already have those. I took down the names and numbers of every guest who's ever stayed at the Sanguine Spa."

"Is that . . . allowed?"

"Oh, definitely not. Should I call them to come rescue us?"

"Yes—" Alexander started, but then Theo held up a hand.

"No. First of all, I can take the tunnels again and open up that door in about two minutes."

"Even without Lucy? What if you get lost?" Alexander was terrified of being lost in a small, dark place.

"I won't. Trust me. Second of all, these grown-ups have already willingly spent days separated from their *own* kids. They're not going to care about someone else's. The Count will just tell them that we were breaking the rules and so he put us in here for our own safety, or some nonsense like that. And they'll believe him because he's a grown-up. And we're kids."

"And I'm a teenager." Wil glowered. "No one believes us, or trusts us, or gives us access to vital records unless we hack into their computer systems in the middle of the night and take them for ourselves."

"You *what?*" Alexander asked.

"What? Nothing. Okay, who should I call, then?"

"The parents. But tell them there's an emergency, and they have to meet you at the hedge maze. Take them to the door we saw in the woods."

"What door?" Wil asked. She hadn't been paying attention.

"Remember the place where we almost made you drop Rodrigo because we saved you from walking off a cliff?"

"Oh, that place! Got it."

"But she has to get through the hedge maze!" Alexander said. "And she has to do it two minutes after Mina does so she doesn't run into them. Theo, can you draw her a map?"

"No need," Wil said, waving Rodrigo. "I downloaded the original landscaping plans. I can use those."

"I'm off, then!" Theo scrambled up the wall and through the tunnels. She couldn't figure out how to get to the coffin closet from this starting point—the tunnels weren't all connected—but she did know exactly where she could get. After a series of corners and ladders, Theo shouted, "Aha!"

She unhooked a latch, then pushed. The painting that

had haunted Alexander swung open on its hinges. Theo had been right about the draft coming from it.

She jumped into the hall and ran straight back up to the library, releasing her siblings. Wil hurried away to meet up with the parents, her phone timer synced to Theo's stopwatch.

"Where are we going?" Alexander asked Theo, following her.

"To the kitchen, and then to get the other kids."

"What's the plan?" Usually, Alexander was the one who made plans, but Theo seemed very excited.

"You know how people are irrationally prejudiced against vampire bats?"

"Yes."

"And usually, we would try not to reinforce those incorrect ideas about how vampire bats are dangerous?"

Alexander, finally understanding, started laughing. "Oh, yes. I see. But how are we going to beat Edgaren't and the Count? Even with Mina leading them astray, we still have to gather everyone and then somehow make it there before them. They have a huge head start!"

"We're not going through the maze. In fact, we're not going outside at all." Theo reached into her pocket and retrieved a heavy key that looked like it belonged to a doorknob that looked like a screaming face. "We're going to find more than one thing that was lost. The catacombs! Which I suspect include a tunnel."

"That's how they kept the lab a secret from the Count! He would have noticed them constantly leaving to do their research and work. But they never set foot outside of the hotel—that he saw." Alexander beamed.

"Now we just have to get the other kids." Theo took off down the hall, and they burst into the kitchen.

Luck was finally on their side. Eris and the Js were lined up at the counter, all somber and sad-looking as they assembled peanut-butter-and-jelly sandwiches. But since there was neither peanut butter nor jelly, they were just bread sandwiches.

"Oh, thank goodness!" Eris said. "Alexander, please, cook for us. We're begging you. The only other things to eat are those terrible smoothies."

Ren was also there, sitting in a chair. Which was surprising because Alexander and Theo really hadn't expected him to be willing to help make meals. And, even more surprising, the two sticky toddlers were sitting on his lap, bouncing up and down.

But then Theo and Alexander realized Ren was only sitting there because he was literally tied to the chair.

"What are you doing here?" Quincy asked, coming in the door. Before she could do anything, Theo shot out her own lasso, neatly snagging the cowgirl. "Quick, get her other lassos!" she said.

Alexander grabbed them. Theo led Quincy to a chair, then proceeded to tie her in the exact same way she had tied Ren.

"Please," Quincy said. "Let me explain."

Theo crouched in front of her. "You're my friend, and you taught me to lasso, but you also betrayed us. So you can explain after we've saved the day. Not delay us so we can't." She grabbed a piece of bread and put it in Quincy's mouth.

"Hey," Eris said. "That's my sandwich! And why are we tying up Quincy?"

"Did she have you looking for something?" Theo asked. "Something secret?"

Eris frowned, and the Js all mimicked her, closing their mouths.

"Let me guess: She gave you a clue. Flat and rectangular."

"Hey!" Ren said. "She gave me that clue, too! And she told me I was the only one special enough to get it!"

Alexander sighed. "She lied to us. She's been using us

to look for something. Something that the Count wants but that would hurt Mina. So now we need your help to help Mina."

"No!" Ren shouted. "I'm still going to win! This is a trick so you can find it before I do. I'm going to win, and my dad's going to be proud of me! Quincy promised!"

Quincy's shoulders drooped, and she lowered her head, ashamed.

Theo crouched in front of Ren. Her first instinct was to tell him she didn't want his help anyway. But she had just been dealing with two bullies, and she didn't want to be one, too. Alexander was used to getting positive praise. Adults loved him. Teachers, crossing guards, grocery store clerks, it didn't matter. They all loved Alexander. Theo, however, didn't receive that same level of universal adoration. A few of her teachers hadn't liked her much, which still hurt her feelings. Fortunately, her last few teachers had understood the way she needed to get instructions broken down, and that sometimes she just had to bounce in her chair. It made a world of difference, having a teacher who saw who she was and appreciated her.

So, even though she didn't necessarily like Ren, she understood him in a way Alexander couldn't. Ren needed someone to *see* him and appreciate him. He was always competitive because he was desperate for praise.

Theo held his gaze. "You need to win so your dad will notice you, right? I know how it feels when the people you want to spend time with aren't around. It hurts. And it's confusing." This summer had taught her that. The two people she could always count on—besides Alexander, of course—were gone. "I don't think winning any competitions here is going to get your dad to notice you. I think he's maybe forgotten how much you need him, but we can remind him of that. Either way, you deserve to be seen and loved for exactly who you are, and I'm sorry I wasn't nicer to you. So will you help us?"

Ren's chin trembled. "You promise my dad will notice me?"

"Oh," Theo said, grinning as she untied Ren while Alexander grabbed the supplies from the cupboards and Quincy watched them all with wide, mournful eyes and a fully breaded mouth, "I can guarantee it."

CHAPTER
THIRTY-SEVEN

Alexander felt like he was holding his breath. He wasn't—in fact, he was breathing quite hard from their sprint down the stairs, through a tunnel, and then tiptoeing through the cave so as not to disturb the tiny brown masses above their heads. But his nerves made it feel like he hadn't breathed in minutes.

Eris and the Js held their noses but demonstrated excellent stealth. Ren stomped, but only because he didn't know any other way to walk, and fortunately the cave floor didn't make too much noise. Theo had tied the two sticky toddlers to her back and wore them like a backpack. It was the only way to keep them from doing something horrible, like licking the walls. Alexander passed the jar around to each kid, doing touch-ups where needed. They were ready.

Theo checked her timer. "Time's almost up," she whispered.

The door at the top of the stairs, the one Mina would lead the Count and Edgaren't to, was still shut. Thank goodness. "Up there!" Alexander whispered, which was difficult with his mouth so full. All the kids made it to the top of the stairs just as the door swung open, throwing sunshine on them like a spotlight.

Mina, the Count, and Edgaren't stood there, each face well and truly shocked as nine children stumbled out of the cave, groaning, with white marshmallow-flavored goop foaming around and out of their mouths.

"What's wrong with them?" the Count asked, tripping as he tried to sweep backward like the world's most surprised broom.

"Rabies?" Mina asked, puzzled. Alexander winked at her. Catching on, she said it again, this time with exaggerated shock and horror. "*Rabies!* Oh no. They've been infected. We can't go down there!"

"Rabies." Edgaren't narrowed his eyes. "I don't think—"

"Rabies?!" shouted Ren's father from the path through the trees. "You gave my son *rabies*?" He pushed past the

Count and Edgaren't, kneeling next to Ren. "What have you been doing with our children?"

"Our babies!" the parents of the two sticky toddlers cried out, rushing forward. Theo tugged on a single knot, and the whole system came undone, dropping the tiny terrors into their parents' waiting arms. "Tied to another child, given rabies, and stickier than ever! Is this what you call children's entertainment?"

The Count took a step back, holding up his hands. "Allow me to explain."

"Our darlings!" Josephine and Josie said, grabbing Eris and the Js and shooting death glares at the Count. "What have you done?"

"Exactly what you wanted me to!" the Count shouted. "You were all perfectly willing to give up your children and ignore them so you could finally get a break. And I gave that to you! Special essential oils to keep you calm and sleepy; meditation to keep you stuck in your own heads where you wouldn't worry about your children; my special smoothies, which we'll have a meeting about soon. All your own needs met first for once. You haven't even thought about these kids! I gave you exactly what you wanted—a break from being parents—and now *I'm* going to get what *I* want."

"You'll never get the bats!" Mina shouted.

"Bats?" Edgaren't asked, his heavy brow furrowing and his frowning mustache still frowning, but in a confused way.

"You aren't after the bats?" Theo asked, wiping away the Marshmallow Fluff. She had never thought she could get sick of that sugary sweetness, but holding it that long in her mouth had made her reconsider. She wasn't going to break up permanently with Marshmallow Fluff, but she definitely needed some time apart.

"Bats? What bats?" the Count said. "I want the real will!"

"Right here," Wil said, standing behind the parents, tapping furiously on her phone.

"No, *W-I-L-L,* as in the legal document determining who owns the Sanguine Spa in the absence of the Blood parents. I need it so that I can—" The Count stopped, a nervous smile peeling apart his red, red lips. "I mean, of course I have the legal will. That's why I'm in charge. That's why everything here is mine. Obviously. And that's why I'm selling the Sanguine Spa to start my own health drink company. The health drink you've all been enjoying this week, which I'll let you get in on the ground floor for! If each of you sells a subscription to everyone you

284

know, then you'll be rich! And I'll be richer!" He smiled that terrible fruit-punch-lips-and-too-many-teeth smile. "And no one here can contest that the spa isn't mine to sell."

A hand shot out of the dark of the cave stairs behind the twins. Lucy was back there, in the shadows, holding a cream-colored envelope with an old-fashioned wax seal in the shape of—unsurprisingly—a bat.

"Lucy?" the Count said, taking another step backward. "You're *here*?"

Alexander grabbed the will and opened it, reading quickly. His eyes got wider and wider as he did. He had learned his lesson at Fathoms of Fun, that one should always read the fine print. This will was nothing but fine print, and it was all the absolute finest print he could have asked for. "This says that if anything happens to the Bloods or if they disappear, everything in, around, and *under* the Sanguine Spa belongs to Mina and Lucy, and that Mina is Lucy's legal guardian. I don't see your name here, anywhere, Count."

"So you can't sell anything." Mina clasped her hands with joy. "Including those terrible smoothies, made with supplies from *my* spa!"

"If you need a good lawyer, Mina," Josephine said,

putting her arm around her wife's shoulders, "Josie here is the best in the Little Transylvanian Mountains."

"But wait. Who are you?" Ren's dad demanded, staring at Edgaren't.

"I'm just here for reading material and to pick up the unattended children," Edgaren't said with a mustachioed smile.

Mina stepped between him and the Sinister-Winterbottom twins. "They're not unattended. They're guests of the hotel, which makes them my guests, which puts me in charge of them."

Josie, the best lawyer in the Little Transylvanian Mountains, gathered up her four children. "I'm going to make things right, for *all* of you children." She smiled at Mina, who, in spite of her responsibilities and maturity, was still only a teenager after all. A lawyer would be a very big help indeed.

"And you!" Ren's dad said, grabbing the Count by his long, cape-like jacket. "You're coming with us. Not only am I not joining your health drink scam, I want a refund. I need to take my son on a *real* family vacation."

Ren beamed. He met Theo's eyes. He tried to scowl out of habit, but he couldn't manage it, so he and Theo just nodded at each other, at last reaching a truce.

"We want a refund, too!" the other parents chimed in. "And to be unsubscribed from that email list you signed us up for without our permission! We should have known you were evil." They marched the Count back toward the caspatle.

Mina took the hand of one of the two sticky toddlers since their parents were busy chasing the other one, who had managed to put a slug in her mouth. "We have a lot of fun to catch up on now that I'm in charge. Are you two coming?" She looked at Alexander and Theo with a smile.

"Yeah. We have a former friend to untie, and an explanation to get." Theo wished this ending were perfectly happy, but, as with most things in life, it was complicated.

"Well then, let's go, because I DON'T WANT TO SEE YOU SET FOOT OUTSIDE THAT DOOR!" Mina walked back toward the caspatle.

Alexander turned and saw Lucy, where, thanks to Mina's shouting, she continued to lurk safely inside the shadows of the cave entrance door. He smiled. "Thanks for the save with the will."

"Yeah, I'm right here," Wil said, wandering closer, eyes on Rodrigo. "I got the parents, like you asked." She frowned at whatever the screen was telling her.

"We noticed," Theo said.

"While you were getting the parents, we got rabies," Alexander said.

"From vampire bats," Theo added.

"We're going to suck your blood," Alexander finished.

Wil nodded. "Yeah, good job," she said. "Now, about—" She finally looked up. Her un-phoned eyes went wide with shock and fear. Not because she finally saw the fake-rabies mess around Theo and Alexander's faces, but because of what Wil *didn't* see.

"Where did he go?" Wil shouted, turning in a circle.

"The parents dragged the Count away to get refunds," Theo said. Wil really needed to pay more attention.

"No, not him. The man who has our books!"

Alexander whirled, looking, but Edgaren't was nowhere to be seen.

CHAPTER
THIRTY-EIGHT

"Back to the hotel!" Alexander shouted, and displaying no caution whatsoever, he threw himself down the stairs, through the cave, through the laboratory, and back up into the hotel, bursting free from the no longer locked door with Theo hot on his heels. They raced up the winding stairs and down the hall to where they had taken the Van H. trunk, but the door was open. The trunk was gone. Edgaren't was gone.

And so were the locked books.

"He never wanted the bats," Alexander said. "Or the will."

"What business does he have with those books? And how did he know we were here?"

Theo pressed her face against the window. Down on the driveway, a girl loaded the last of the books—the Sinister book—into the trunk of a car. Then she shut it, looking up at them. Her lasso waved a sad goodbye as she climbed into a car with Edgaren't, and they sped away.

"I thought she was our friend. Why would she help him?" Theo wished she could send her bees out as an attacking force. They had no way to get to Edgaren't, no way to catch up or know where he was going with their books. In fit of rage, Theo kicked over the trash can. Several wadded-up pieces of paper rolled free, along with a few crumpled and empty raisin snack boxes. Truly evil.

Alexander noticed a shiny brochure among the trash. He picked it up. It was a guide for a summer camp. And on it, in brutal, messy handwriting, someone had written a date for next week, along with:

Reservation for four

W. Sinister-Winterbottom

T. Sinister-Winterbottom

A. Sinister-Winterbottom

Q. Van Helsing

"Quincy's last name is Van Helsing?" Theo asked, confused about why she would have the same name as Edgaren't. If that even was Edgaren't's name.

"Her uncle," Alexander said. "He finally came. Edgaren't is Quincy's *uncle*."

"Why did he make reservations for us? Do you think that's where he's taking the books?"

"There's only one way to find out." Alexander was scared but determined. He couldn't believe that Quincy was evil. He wouldn't believe it. After all, they were willing to steal things for Aunt Saffronia, and they barely knew her. If Aunt Saffronia was secretly evil, maybe they'd be doing bad things, too, thinking they were doing the right thing.

He wanted those books back, and he wanted a chance to talk to Quincy. And probably apologize for helping tie her up.

"Come on," Alexander said. "Let's find Wil."

Theo glared out the glass. "This was the worst vacation ever."

"Well," Alexander said, "you did rappel down that cliff to get me out of the cave when the door shut."

"That's true," Theo said. That had been exciting.

"And you did navigate both a hedge maze *and* a maze of tunnels through the whole caspatle."

"That's also true."

"And going outside in that much humidity was basically the same as swimming."

Theo laughed. "Okay, true enough."

"*And* we got to hunt vampires. Even if they turned out to be really sweet and helpful vampire bats. How many kids can say that about their summer vacations?"

Theo nodded. "I guess this wasn't a total waste. And we made new friends, too." She thought of Ren and hoped he'd find a way to be happier. She thought of Eris and the Js and hoped they'd have a better vacation. She thought of the two sticky toddlers and hoped they'd take a bath.

And she thought of Quincy and didn't know what she hoped, because she was still too mad.

They went to find Wil, but she was already waiting for them in the lobby with their suitcases at her feet and her own bag slung over her shoulder. "Aunt Saffronia's here," Wil snapped, clutching her phone to her chest. "I don't know how she knew."

"Knew what?" Alexander asked.

"That we were done. I can't believe he got the books." She scowled.

"He got the books, but we have . . ." Theo pulled the key ring out of her pocket, jingling it in front of Wil. Wil's eyes left Rodrigo and lit up.

"Oh, you absolutely brilliant, wonderful little twerps!" Wil crushed them both into a hug. "Well done."

"We also have—" Alexander went to get the magnifying glass, but his fingers closed around the letter instead. He pulled it out. "Here. Mom left this for us. It's not very helpful." He passed it to Wil. She read it with narrowed eyes, her lips moving with the words.

"Gather the tools," she whispered. "And . . . use my phone?"

Alexander shrugged. "We don't know why she thought that was helpful, either. Now will you tell us what's going on, and why you called yourself Wil-o'-the-Wisp on the phone, and who you were threatening to destroy, and how you knew about those books, and why you—"

Wil's phone chimed with a text, and she let them go, lost to Rodrigo once more. "Use my phone. Use my phone? Use my phone. Hmm."

Mina rushed into the lobby before Alexander and Theo could get mad at Wil. "Oh, thank you! I couldn't have done any of this without you. And now I can finally run the spa the way my parents wanted, and keep Lucy out in the open, and take care of my bats and continue the research."

"I know your parents would be proud of you," Alexander said. "I'm so sorry you lost them."

"Oh, we didn't *lose* them," Mina said, frowning. "They were taken."

"What?"

"I just mean WHY DON'T YOU LISTEN WHEN I TELL YOU SOMETHING THE FIRST TIME!" Mina shouted, but then she wrapped Alexander up in a hug. "I'm so sorry, I've got to go, so much to do, thanks to you two."

Alexander felt his face burning, and he couldn't remember what he had been asking about because Mina was so very pretty and smelled so very nice.

She hugged Theo next, but Theo was also distracted, trying to see what Lucy was up to, and jealous that she hadn't gotten much of a chance to climb around the rafters with the little girl. Then Mina was hurrying away into the spa that was now well and truly hers.

"Aunt Saffronia's here." Wil stepped out into the sunshine. Theo and Alexander followed. Behind them they heard Mina shouting for Lucy to not dare do whatever it was she was about to do. They turned around to see Lucy hanging back in the shadow of the door, almost but not quite touching the sunlight.

Theo and Alexander raised their hands to wave goodbye. But they froze as Lucy finally smiled all the way, and they realized this whole time they had never seen her talk. She'd only spoken to them in the dark, and she had never smiled. Almost like she'd been keeping a secret in her mouth.

"Are those *fangs?*" Alexander asked, but Aunt Saffronia's car was suddenly in front of them. Wil ushered them inside and slammed the doors before they could protest. Alexander and Theo pushed their faces against the glass, but they couldn't see Lucy or her tiny vampire fangs anymore.

Aunt Saffronia hit the gas, and they surged away, turning the land around them into a blur of green. "We can look closer now," Aunt Saffronia said.

Alexander squeaked with dismay as he reached into his pocket and pulled out the magnifying glass. He hadn't asked Mina permission to take it!

"Aggressive borrowing," Theo reminded him before he could feel too bad. "Besides, it was part of our family's book."

Aunt Saffronia stared out the window. But not the windshield. The side window. The car didn't seem to need her to look where she was going, even though Alexander very much wanted her to.

"Don't you want to hear how our vacation was?" Theo asked.

"I know everything I need to. Though I'm afraid there's still so much for you children to discover. So much to be done."

Wil grunted, scowling at her phone. "I'll find them," she whispered to herself.

"We're going to the seaside," Aunt Saffronia declared. "To find what—"

"No," Alexander said, surprising them all with how confidently he contradicted an adult. He really was changing. "We're going to summer camp. This one." He held the brochure out.

Aunt Saffronia went even paler, if such a thing was possible. She was nearly translucent now. "You aren't ready."

"Ready for what?" Theo asked.

"Ready to face summer camp."

Alexander suddenly remembered the title of that book he had seen, and regretted his bravery. "Is this camp . . . ? Would you say it's in a mountainous lake region?"

"Oh, yes, certainly." Aunt Saffronia nodded somberly.

"I think we can handle it," Theo said. After all, they had braved underwater caves and solved the mystery of the missing Widow at Fathoms of Fun, and they had protected vampires and restored the caspatle to its rightful owners at the Sanguine Spa. What was summer camp compared to those?

"I don't care where we go," Wil muttered, "as long as there's Wi-Fi and I can get those books back."

"Very well," Aunt Saffronia said, her voice distorting. "If this is what you want. Though I cannot guarantee your happiness or safety."

"Come on, it's a summer camp," Theo said. "Even if Edgaren't is there, what's the worst that can happen? Poison ivy?"

"No," Aunt Saffronia said, shaking her head solemnly. "You're going to dye."

"What?" Theo and Alexander gasped in unison.

"Tie-dye. A lot of tie-dye. Be careful of the twists. . . ."

The twins slumped, relieved and tired. "At least we know it can't possibly be battier than this vacation," Theo said, grinning.

Alexander laughed. "Trading summer vamps for summer camps seems like a good choice."

It did seem like a good choice, didn't it?

But they would soon find they had no choices whatsoever, and some camps took tying . . . and dying . . . deadly seriously.

Acknowledgments

Oh, hello! Thank you so much for joining the Sinister-Winterbottoms on another adventurously terrible adventure. I hope your own summer vacations have significantly fewer mean mustaches and absolutely no multilevel marketing health drink scams. But I hope they do have adventures and friends and family. And maybe even a vampire or two, just to keep things interesting.

My own adventurous friends and family help tremendously to get these books out of my head and into yours. My agent, Michelle Wolfson, has been my friend and business partner for a dozen years now, and never minds when I get a little too scary for her. My editor, Wendy Loggia, and her intrepid assistant editor, Ali Romig, helped me figure out exactly what a vampire spa might be like, and guided the story down a slug-strewn path, through a maze, and out the other side. Kristopher Kam, publicity phenom, is always there to deviously plot how to get my books into as many hands as possible, and the entire marketing and publicity team at Delacorte Press and Get Underlined are so delightful I'd lasso them to a chair just to hang out with them for a while. (Except I have neither a lasso nor a chair big enough for everyone, which are two huge oversights on my part.) My copy editor, Jackie Hornberger, is so smart and wonderful, I'd want her on my team in any scavenger hunt, whether through a bat-infested hotel or an old graveyard, or, as is most likely, a manuscript where the scavenger hunt is "find all the ways Kiersten doesn't know how to use commas or dashes" and the prize at the end is doing it all over again for the next book. Finally, if you, like Alexander, judge books by their covers, you can join me in thanking Hannah Peck for illustrating such a phenomenal cover, and Carol Ly for designing it.

In addition to people whose job it is to work with me are many wonderful people who don't get paid to figure out why, exactly, I hate raisins so much, but who choose to spend their time with me anyway. Stephanie Perkins and Natalie Whipple are behind the scenes of everything I write, encouraging, supporting, and otherwise being on my team in every way imaginable. I've been married to my best friend for twenty years now, and his joyful interest in the world around us is a constant inspiration.

Our three kids keep me grounded without ever needing to be grounded themselves, as they are all responsible to a degree that's almost spooky. I'm so glad I get to be their mom, and that I have yet to mysteriously disappear and leave them with an unknown aunt.

There's always next summer, though. . . .

And finally, to Kimberly, our backyard dinosaur, who did nothing to deserve to be in these acknowledgments but is in them anyway.

About the Author

KIERSTEN WHITE has never been a lifeguard, camp counselor, or churro stand operator, and in fact has never once experienced summer or summer vacation or solved any mysteries during the aforementioned season. Anyone saying otherwise is lying, and you should absolutely not listen to them, even if they offer you a churro. *Especially* if they offer you a churro.

Though she was never a lifeguard, camp counselor, or churro stand operator, Kiersten is the *New York Times* bestselling author of more than twenty books, including *Beanstalker and Other Hilarious Scarytales*. She lives with her family near the beach and keeps all her secrets safely buried in her backyard, where they are guarded by a ferocious tortoise named Kimberly.

Visit her at kierstenwhite.com, or check out sinistersummer.com for clues about what awaits the Sinister-Winterbottoms in their next adventure.

JOIN THE SINISTER-WINTERBOTTOM
TWINS ON THEIR NEXT ADVENTURE IN

SINISTER SUMMER

CAMP CREEPY

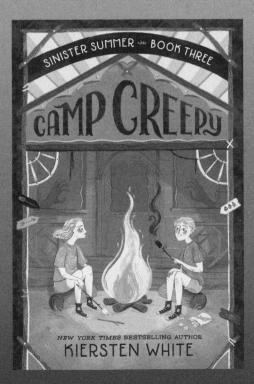

CHAPTER
ONE

The Sinister-Winterbottoms had a problem.
Well, they had several problems. Their parents had dropped them off with a previously unknown— and seriously weird—aunt in the middle of the night and then disappeared. Sixteen-year-old Wil, twelve-year-old Theo, and also twelve-year-old Alexander had not heard from their parents once since then, other than a frustratingly vague letter.

There was a man with small, mean eyes and a large, mean mustache who kept turning up where they didn't want him. Which, to be fair, was a long list of places. Basically everywhere imaginable was a place they didn't want to see Edgaren't. The only places they might be happy to see him were: behind bars, in a pit with unclimbable walls, or at the DMV, a terrible place adults went to be tormented.

They had first met Edgaren't and his large, mean mustache at Fathoms of Fun Waterpark, where he had tried to steal the whole park. Then again at the Sanguine Spa, where he succeeded in stealing a locked book with their name on it. *And* there was a chance Edgaren't had been intending to steal them as well.

Currently, they were on their way to a camp where he might be lurking, which had seemed important when they left. Track him down, get their book back, and find out why their former friend Quincy was helping him. Somehow, especially to Alexander, going where they knew Edgaren't might be didn't feel like the best idea now that it was actually happening.

But, even with this abundance of problems, there was one problem that was quickly leaping to the top of their already-high problem pile: Aunt Saffronia's car wasn't working. More specifically, it seemed to be ... disappearing.

"This car wasn't a convertible when we got in, was it?" Theo stared upward in consternation, a word she liked because it was like confusion had populated an entire nation. There had definitely been a normal, solid car roof above them at the beginning of the drive. And now there was only sky.

"That's weird," Alexander said.

"Which part?" Theo answered, gesturing to everything around them.

"No wind."

He had a point. There was no breeze. It was like they were sealed in against the world. But the boundaries of that seal were dissolving. Even the windows seemed less solid than they had a few minutes before.

Theo was very brave—sometimes to the point of being reckless, though she was trying to be reckful whenever possible now—but she drew the line at speeding down a lonely, empty forest road in a car that wasn't sure whether or not it wanted to keep existing.

"It was *not* a convertible when we got in." Alexander was sure of it. He wouldn't have gotten into a convertible, worrying that there was no roof above him if the car were to flip or if an aggressive hawk were to take a liking to his hair. He had nice hair, always neatly parted and combed, and he could imagine exactly what it would feel like for a hawk to sink its greedy talons in.

Unlike his twin, he was not very brave, and never reckless or even reckful, preferring tremendous caution in all things. He was thoughtful and careful and deeply, deeply worried. As a default, but particularly at the current moment.

It had been bad enough heading toward a camp where Edgaren't might be waiting for them. Worse, too, that Alexander suspected it was the same camp he had seen a book about. A book entitled *A History of Summer Camps and the Unexplained Disappearances of Various Campers in the Mountainous Lake Regions*. Worst that they were doing it in a car that wasn't dependable.

Their dad knew a lot about mechanics on account of building battle robots in their garage all the time. He would agree that a dependable car had a reliable engine in good working order *and* a body that didn't disappear at random.

Alexander watched the mountainous landscape with dread, waiting for a lake to appear. He should have broken rules for once and aggressively borrowed that book from the Sanguine Spa library. At least then he'd know what they were getting into. Surely their friend Mina, who owned the spa now thanks to their help, wouldn't have held it against him.

Sometimes reading was a necessary survival skill. And Alexander really wanted to survive.

Wil should have had an opinion about the state of the car, but she was too busy staring at Rodrigo. Rodrigo, its case covered in shiny stickers, was her constant companion. But it was the shine of its screen that held a magnetic grip on both Wil's eyes and her brain.

"Here, twerp," she said, holding her hand out. "Let me be in charge of the keys to the books until we find them."

Alexander was more than happy to relinquish the ring of tiny keys he had gotten from Lucy's nest. Holding on to the keys meant being responsible for them, and even though he was the most responsible twelve-year-old possibly in existence, he didn't *want* to be responsible for something so important.

"About the car," he said, hoping Aunt Saffronia would reassure them. But instead, as though triggered by their doubts, the car drifted to a stop.

"What's wrong?" Alexander asked. They were surrounded by towering trees so green they were nearly black. The road beneath them was cracked with disuse. It didn't look like anyone was around for miles and miles.

Aunt Saffronia stayed in the driver's seat, gripping the steering wheel. "I can't go any further," she informed them.

"So the car *is* breaking." Theo was glad to have it confirmed, even if she had never heard of a car breaking down by slowly evaporating. It didn't seem like an overly car-ish thing to do. Then again, it was their father who was mechanically minded. So maybe he'd have an explanation, if he had bothered to stick with them this summer.

Theo glared out the window. But that wasn't quite right. She lifted her hand and held it straight through where the window no longer was. Theo glared out the empty space that wasn't a window anymore.

This was all their parents' fault, and she was mad at them for being gone. Being mad was easier than being worried about where they were, why they had gone, why they hadn't come back or even called. Why there had been a book with their family name on it at the Sanguine Spa's secret hidden library, and why a mean mustachioed man would want that book and the six others like it.

Alexander found it easy to be worried enough for the both of them, though. His worry was always generous that way. He was sure his mom could have reassured him, would have laughed and declared this all an adventure while passing out cookies she miraculously produced from her depthless purse. But she wasn't here, and unlike Theo, Alexander wasn't mad at all. He was just scared.

And he *really* wanted a book to distract himself with.

Two books, ideally. Both the Sinister family book and the book about camp disappearances.

Wil looked up, taking in their surroundings with a frown. If she noticed huge portions of the car were missing, she didn't indicate it. "Come on, Aunt Saff, we have to get there. I *need* to get those books."